"I have something for you."

Chaz pulled out a beautiful one-carat diamond set in yellow gold. "This isn't real, but you wouldn't know it without a jeweler's loupe."

In a daze, Lacey took the ring from him. The reality of it sent her thoughts back to the night Ted had promised to love her till the day he died. Her darling husband—he'd died way too soon.

Now here she was with a fake engagement ring handed to her by this remarkable PI while he tried to find out who was stalking her. She felt as though she was living some strange dream.

"Once we catch your stalker—which will happen before long—you can tell everyone the truth and they'll all understand the reason for the deception."

Lacey couldn't believe she'd agreed to this arrangement with a virtual stranger, but Chaz was the expert and everything he'd said had made a certain kind of sense. If she didn't have faith in him, then what else was there?

Dear Reader,

My Undercover Heroes series started a few years ago in Harlequin Superromance. The hero in the first book, *Undercover Husband,* was Roman Lufka, who headed his own PI firm. Now, a few years later, he appears in Harlequin American Romance and has hired three more PIs to work for him.

The first book in this new series is *The SEAL's Promise.* Chaz Roylance is a former navy SEAL who bears a heavy burden he can't shake until he's hired to track down Lacey Pomeroy's stalker. I won't go into the details, but it might interest you to know that of all the heroines I've created (110 so far) she, more than the others, has a lot of the real *moi* in her.

Enjoy!

Rebecca Winters

The SEAL's Promise

REBECCA WINTERS

TORONTO NEW YORK LONDON
AMSTERDAM PARIS SYDNEY HAMBURG
STOCKHOLM ATHENS TOKYO MILAN MADRID
PRAGUE WARSAW BUDAPEST AUCKLAND

ISBN-13: 978-0-373-75391-8

THE SEAL'S PROMISE

ABOUT THE AUTHOR

Rebecca Winters, whose family of four children has now swelled to include five beautiful grandchildren, lives in Salt Lake City, Utah, in the land of the Rocky Mountains. With canyons and high alpine meadows full of wildflowers, she never runs out of places to explore. They, plus her favorite vacation spots in Europe, often end up as backgrounds for her romance novels, because writing is her passion, along with her family and church. Rebecca loves to hear from readers. If you wish to email her, please visit her website at www.cleanromances.com.

Books by Rebecca Winters

HARLEQUIN AMERICAN ROMANCE

1261—THE CHIEF RANGER
1275—THE RANGER'S SECRET
1302— A MOTHER'S WEDDING DAY
    "A Mother's Secret"
1310—WALKER: THE RODEO LEGEND
1331—SANTA IN A STETSON
1339—THE BACHELOR RANGER
1367—RANGER DADDY
1377—A TEXAS RANGER'S CHRISTMAS

HARLEQUIN SUPERROMANCE

1034—BENEATH A TEXAS SKY
1065—SHE'S MY MOM
1112—ANOTHER MAN'S WIFE
1133—HOME TO COPPER MOUNTAIN
1210—WOMAN IN HIDING
1233—TO BE A MOTHER
1259—SOMEBODY'S DAUGHTER
1282—THE DAUGHTER'S RETURN

HARLEQUIN ROMANCE

4148—CINDERELLA ON HIS DOORSTEP
4172—MIRACLE FOR THE GIRL NEXT DOOR
4185—DOORSTEP TWINS
4191—ACCIDENTALLY PREGNANT!
4219—THE NANNY AND THE CEO
4239—HER DESERT PRINCE
4244—AND BABY MAKES THREE
    "Adopted Baby, Convenient Wife"

This book is dedicated to Art Bell, whose nationally syndicated radio call-in program about all things inexplicable entertained me for years.

Chapter One

Since moving to Salt Lake a year ago, former Navy SEAL Chaz Roylance had developed a craving for the glazed donuts sold at SweetSpuds on Foothill Drive. They were better than any other donuts he'd ever eaten. He'd discovered that the small store wasn't that far from his work.

After buying a dozen for the guys, he headed for the Lufka P.I. firm located farther south where Foothill Drive turned into Wasatch Boulevard. Mount Olympus provided the backdrop. As Chaz pulled around the back past the shop filled with their equipment, he realized no man could ask for a more glorious setting, especially on a warm summer morning with a clear blue sky overhead.

In fact, no man worked with better guys or a more brilliant boss. Roman Lufka owned the agency and was great to work for. Chaz's P.I. job forced him to concentrate on other people's problems and blot out his own for a while. He dealt with lots of missing-persons cases, embezzlement and industrial espionage.

But lately he'd reached a point where the disease eating away at his soul was taking over again. He'd been losing sleep and didn't know the meaning of joy.

He felt it particularly strongly this morning because he'd just finished solving an insurance-fraud case—not a good place for him to be since it gave him too much thinking time.

After parking his green Forerunner in his space, he entered the office through the back door and nodded to Lisa Gordon, an ex-cop and Roman's assistant, who was making coffee in the kitchen. "I was counting on the java being ready."

She eyed his sack of donuts. "Hmm. I had hopes someone would bring me breakfast."

"Here. Take one. We make a good team, Lisa."

"That we do. Thanks." She flashed him a searching glance and put her hands on her hips. "You don't look so good. I know what's wrong with you. All work and no play makes Jack a dull boy. You need a little fun in your life. How about letting me introduce you to this very attractive brunette accountant who's a friend of my daughter."

"No, thanks, but I appreciate the offer."

She studied him with concern. "Maybe you need some professional help for what's ailing you."

"Maybe."

"I recognize the signs because I've been there."

Wrong. Even as an ex-cop, she hadn't been where he'd been. Certain work he'd had to do in the SEALs shouldn't be part of the human experience. He flashed her a jaundiced eye, then picked up a coffee before heading to Roman's office.

Lisa, the mother of two whose last child had just gone away to college, never quit when it came to Chaz. She and her husband had a tight marriage. So did Roman. Before cancer had taken Chaz's wife ten years ago, he'd been happy, too, but her death had changed his life and had prompted him to join the military, where he'd ultimately become a navy SEAL.

The work had been challenging and he'd enjoyed the camaraderie well enough. Then came his last mission in South America with Special Forces, where he'd come up against something that had torn him apart. The warlords forced their women to carry out their atrocities. Chaz's orders were to kill them, but the very thought of killing women went against everything he believed in. He couldn't do it and realized it was time to get out.

Since then, nightmares had plagued him. With his parents dead and his wife gone, there was nothing for him to go back to in Arizona, where he'd been born and raised. Desperate to find meaning in his life, he'd moved to Salt Lake. He'd taken his wife to the Huntsman Institute there for her last two months of cancer treatment.

He'd liked the city well enough, and there was an opportunity for work in a civilian setting that needed his intelligence-gathering skills. Roman's P.I. firm kept him constantly busy in an environment that gave him purpose without destroying him.

"Roman?" he called from the doorway. "You busy?"

"You're the man I wanted to see this morning. Come on in."

Chaz sat down, sharing the goodies with him.

"Thank you. Much more of this and Brittany's going to put me on a diet."

Anyone looking at Roman, who stayed in great shape, would think he was in his late thirties instead of mid-forties. He and his brother Yuri came from Russian roots and grew up in New York. They were both dark haired with fascinating personalities.

"Congratulations for winding up that insurance-fraud case so fast, comrade. Planting the camera was a master stroke. The guys cracked up when they watched the film. I did, too, when I saw the paralyzed guy get out of his bed and start walking around the minute the door was closed." He broke into laughter and consumed his donut in one swallow.

"It was a lucky hunch that paid off."

Roman eyed him frankly. "All your hunches are lucky, which proves to me it isn't luck with you. The SEALs' loss was my gain, but I've sensed something's been wrong for a while. What can I do to help?"

Chaz grimaced. "I must be transparent. Lisa's trying to find me a woman, convinced it will heal all wounds."

"Brittany changed my life, but since I know love has to happen on its own, I won't go down that path with you. Lisa cares about you. We all do. But I know there's something else. If you ever need to unload, I'm here."

"Thanks. Maybe one day," Chaz murmured. If anyone would get it, Roman would, but Chaz wasn't ready to talk about his troubles yet.

"I'm glad you came in because a dozen new cases need to be assigned. You can have your pick. But before I tell you about them, I wondered if you'd find out if the man who left this number on our answering machine is legitimate." Roman handed him a note with the name Barry Winslow on it.

"What do you mean by legitimate?"

Roman sat forward in his chair. "I mean, I don't know any details, which is a first. It's a Salt Lake area code, but the number's unlisted. If it turns out the call

was some sort of prank, then come back in and we'll
go over the new cases."

"I'll take care of this right now."

*I CAN HARDLY WAIT TO SEE your blood on my hands, you
bitch. So watch out and keep looking over your shoulder, because I'm right behind you and plan to cut
out your freakin' heart first. Then I'll start on your
daughter.... Both will be an in-the-body experience
you won't forget.*

Those horrifying words left in a message on her
cell phone yesterday afternoon stabbed through Lacey
Pomeroy over and over again as she walked her three-
year-old to her bedroom. "Come on, Abby, honey. Time
for your nap."

After Lacey put her daughter under the covers with
her favorite stuffed frog, she lay down on the twin bed
and cuddled her close. While she sang to Abby, she
stared at the ceiling in mortal fear of what was going
on in her life right now. The morning before yesterday,
she'd received the first phoned death threat, but it had
come on her condo's landline.

*Get ready for your next paranormal experience. It'll
happen when you least expect it. This one's going to
burn up your brain. Literally.*

Since then, the landline hadn't rung again. The calls
on both phones had come from the same man. Both
gruesome messages reminded her of the death threat
she'd found before leaving Long Beach, California, and
moving back to Salt Lake a year ago. Salt Lake had
been a safe haven, the place where she'd grown up, and
where her mom and sister still lived.

The death threat had happened the night of the

viewing for her husband, Ted, who'd been in the Coast Guard and had died in an accident at sea.

A big crowd had come to the mortuary in Long Beach to offer their condolences. When she went out to her car later, she found a note put under her windshield wiper. It had said that aliens were responsible for her husband's death. Now they were going to set her daughter on fire one body part at a time before they did the same thing to her.

She'd assumed the depraved monster was a listener of her paranormal radio program that was broadcast out of Los Angeles. After showing the note to her mother and sister, who'd come to Long Beach for the funeral, she'd told her boss about it. He'd assured her it was a sick prank, probably done by some messed-up teenager in her neighborhood who knew her car and had seen the obituary. He'd told her not to worry about it unless she got another one.

But Lacey hadn't waited to find out. With her husband gone, she quit her California radio call-in show. When she moved back home, Barry Winslow, a Salt Lake radio producer, contacted her to do the same show here because it was so popular. She hadn't thought about the note again until she'd gotten that first phone call.

Lacey had never needed her husband more, but Ted had been dead a year. With no father to turn to, she'd called Barry. He wasn't only the head producer for the network sponsoring her radio call-in show here, the married father of three had been like a favorite uncle to her since she'd moved back to Salt Lake.

When she'd told him she was being stalked and gave him proof, he'd taken her seriously, but told her not to try to trace the calls back to their source yet. Since they both knew the police couldn't do anything until some kind of crime had been committed, he'd told her he had an idea and would get back to her today.

Once her daughter was asleep, Lacey got off the bed and walked through the one-story condo to the kitchen. She'd left her cell phone on the counter and was still waiting to hear back from Barry. The window above the sink looked out at the other condos in the Parkridge complex where she lived in Cottonwood Heights. Hers was one of the second-story units in a three-story building that housed six condos. The stalker could be out there watching her condo this very second.

When she'd moved back from California, she'd chosen this place to be near her mother, Virginia Garvey, who taught math part-time at the University of Utah, and lived only a half mile from Lacey's condo. Lacey's sister, Ruth, had been staying with their mom for the past month after losing her job as an air cargo pilot in Idaho. With Ted gone, Lacey had needed her family.

She hoped to make enough money to sell her condo and buy a house in a nearby residential neighborhood by the time Abby was old enough to start kindergarten. In the meantime, twenty-six-year-old Ruth stayed over with her on weeknights and went to their mother's on the weekends.

While Abby slept, Ruth babysat so Lacey could do her three-hour radio show. In return, Lacey paid her well, so her sister didn't have to take a part-time job. Their situation was temporary because Ruth would be getting another job soon, but it had been working out fine. Until two days ago, when some maniac had disrupted their lives!

Lacey's family believed the horrendous threats had to have come from one of her radio show listeners who delighted in frightening her. Maybe it was the same person who'd put that note on her car in California. The possibility that this insane person had followed her here and had been watching all this time terrified her.

The bloodcurdling part for Lacey was the fact that he knew both her phone numbers. On her way home from the park with Abby yesterday, her cell phone had rung. Since she hadn't recognized the caller ID, she hadn't picked up.

When she reached her condo, she was so filled with dread it took her a long time to gather the courage to listen to the voice message. It was the same man's voice, but the death threat had been more violent and graphic. At that point she hadn't hesitated to phone Barry, who'd promised to help her.

Why hadn't he called her yet?

There was no way she would leave the condo to do her show tonight. Barry would have to get Stewart, the nighttime intern producer who also ran the phones, to play another of her taped programs from the archives. She'd told her sister to stay at their mom's tonight.

While she stood in the middle of her kitchen trapped by her thoughts and fears, there was a knock on the front door. She heard her mother's voice and rushed through the living room to open it.

"Thank goodness you're here." She hugged her hard. "I've been going out of my mind waiting for Barry to call."

"Shh," her mother said. After she closed and locked the door, she turned to Lacey. "We have to whisper." Lacey frowned. "Your condo might be bugged."

What?

Her mother led her to the hallway. Still whispering, she said, "Barry isn't going to phone you, honey. Mr. Winslow called a P.I. firm to help you."

Lacey blinked. "Are you serious?"

"Yes. The man in charge of your case is Chaz Roylance. He told Barry not to have any more phone conversations with you. Then he called me."

"You've already talked to this P.I.?"

"I just got off the phone with him. He said the fact that we haven't contacted the police works in our favor. With a high-profile person like you, the minute the police hear, the news will leak to the press and any hope for secrecy will be lost."

"That's true, but isn't it going to cost a lot of money?"

"Barry said the network will pay the expenses. To quote him, 'We're not letting the paranormal-show host with the fourth-highest ratings in the nation be hurt by some fringe lunatic.'"

Lacey's eyelids prickled. "Barry's wonderful."

"I agree. So is this P.I."

"How did he find him?"

"Barry says he's from the top P.I. firm in the Intermountain West, bar none. This Mr. Roylance has already assigned his people to keep you under twenty-four-hour surveillance."

"That fast?" She was incredulous…and grateful.

"Yes. But of course this is your decision. I'm just relating what Barry told me to tell you. If you want to call this off, just say so, honey."

"No, Mom. I know he's doing everything he can for me and I appreciate your help more than you'll ever know. Do you know what I'm supposed to do now?"

"Yes. Mr. Roylance said we're all to stick to our normal routines. You're to keep to the same schedule and go to work tonight. Ruth's planning to come over. Don't answer your phones. If you recognize the caller ID, you can phone people back when you're outside the house, but don't tell a soul what's going on."

Lacey shuddered. "You honestly trust him to know how to handle this?"

"Barry says they're an accredited firm the FBI and the police recommend if you ask them privately. He's had friends who've used them before. They have impeccable credentials. He told me he wouldn't trust anyone else to do this kind of work. Again, it's your decision, but for what it's worth, I trust him."

That was good enough for Lacey. They didn't have another solution right now. "When am I going to meet this P.I.?"

"Mr. Roylance has laid out a plan. Tomorrow night he'll come to the radio station with one of his crew. They'll be disguised as satellite-dish workers sent out by their company. While they pretend to check out the television equipment in the room, he'll talk to you while you're doing your show."

"But I don't take breaks."

"He says he's coordinated this with Barry. Tonight at work you'll announce you're going to play a tape tomorrow night from last year's Summer Solstice Conference in Milwaukee. Barry told him about it and said it would take up a half hour plus the advertisement time.

"When you get to work tomorrow night, you're to tell Stewart to start the tape after the ten o'clock news. Mr. Roylance will come into the broadcast booth then, pretending to check the place out thoroughly. You're to more or less ignore him and behave as you would around any workman.

"He said everyone who *has* or *does* business at the station is suspect, which of course includes Stewart, the night watchman and the janitor, so you shouldn't do anything to alert anyone that this night is different from any other.

"While the tape is playing, it will give him enough time to talk to you without anyone being aware. No one will have a clue what's going on. After talking to Mr. Roylance, I have no doubts he's more than capable of catching this depraved maniac."

Lacey had been listening to her mom. "I couldn't bear it if anything happened to Abby."

"I couldn't, either. Mr. Roylance has assured me they're prepared to intervene in case of trouble and he guarantees your safety. You're to try to relax and go about your business. He'll contact you through me until after he's met with you tomorrow night."

"I—I can't believe this has happened." Her voice shook.

Her mom hugged her again. "I know, but I'll always be indebted to Barry for acting this fast. Mr. Roylance wants you to stay strong and not fall apart. Remember, you're not to discuss this situation with anyone. Let the P.I. do his job. He's convinced me he'll get you through this safely."

"If you believe in him, Mom."

"I do. When you talk to him, you will, too."

Her mother sounded so sure. Lacey wanted to believe it because she was terrified.

THE CALL FROM BARRY WINSLOW had turned out to be the legitimate thing. Once Chaz had verified he was the producer for the Ionosphere Network in Salt Lake and had vetted him for everything he knew, he went back to Roman's office and shut the door. After his boss got off the phone, he looked at Chaz. "What did you find out?"

"It's the real thing. Furthermore, it's a stalking case involving a bona fide celebrity." He filled him in on the details.

Roman whistled when he learned it was Lacey Pomeroy. "A dozen people around here love her show, including Brittany."

"Obviously millions of people do or she wouldn't be ranked fourth in the national paranormal market. Her producer told me her popularity originally sprang from a novel she'd written while still in high school under her maiden name, Garvey. I'm intrigued by everything I've learned and would like to take the case."

"It's yours. Use any backup crew and equipment you need."

"Thanks, Roman. I'll keep you informed."

Whether it turned out to be a hideous prank or the work of a true psychopath didn't matter. Chaz wanted the case for reasons he hadn't fully examined yet. But he sensed that if he found the person stalking this woman and could make her feel safe again, maybe he would sleep better. To prevent a crime against her and her child might ease certain horrific memories.

Mr. Winslow had told him there'd been another death threat in the form of a note while she'd still been living in California. That incident could have been done for a different reason by a different person from the one who'd made these telephone threats. It would be up to Chaz to find out if there was a connection.

Once he'd set up the teams he used on stakeouts

and his people were in place, he called every bookstore trying to find a copy of the book on the paranormal that Lacey Garvey had written. The fiction novel had put her on the map, so to speak, and had been her entry into the world of sci-fi radio.

The bookstores and used bookstores were all sold out. In frustration, he bought the newest electronic reader on the market and downloaded the novel to read when he got home. He preferred a real book in hand, but this would have to do.

Whenever he went to work for a client, he attempted to get to know everything he could about him or her first. This book and her radio program showed where her passions lay and would inevitably be helpful to him if he hoped to get inside her stalker's mind. Tomorrow evening he'd be prepared to talk to her at the radio station.

After giving his crew instructions and coordinating who would be coming off and going on shift, he ate a quick dinner at a drive-thru and headed to his condo building at the mouth of Parley's Canyon. His sixth-floor unit was no home, but it served its purpose and was convenient being right off the freeway and close to his office.

With everything taken care of for the moment, he walked into his bedroom with his purchase. Removing his shoes and ankle holster, he set the alarm for the clock radio to go off at 9:00 p.m., the time her program started. He grabbed some licorice from the bedside table and turned on the lamp.

Finally he was ready to read and lay back on the bed, propping his head with a couple of pillows. He glanced at the title, *The Stargrazer from Algol,* a young-adult fantasy novel by new *New York Times* bestselling author Lacey Garvey, winner of the Hugo Award and the Nebula Award for the best science-fiction fantasy novel.

As he scrolled down, he discovered it had been published ten years ago and was in its seventh printing. He clicked to the back of the book where he saw a black-and-white picture of a pretty girl with long hair that could have been a high school yearbook photo. She'd been only eighteen when this book was published. That meant she'd been writing long before that.

He was impressed someone with a gift like hers had achieved that level of success so early in life.

Chaz scrolled to the dedication. *To my wonderful parents, Virginia and Bill, who've given me life and love.* On the next page was a quote by Robert A. Heinlein, the grand master of science-fiction writers of all time. He'd said something to the effect that supernatural happenings might seem as if they were in the realm of magic or fantasy, but in truth, they followed the lines of engineering and made what some people called impossible possible.

He remembered reading an assigned story in a junior high English class written by Heinlein. As Chaz recalled, it was about some college-age guy and his physicist uncle who'd flown a rocket to the moon where they'd found someone had arrived there first. It was pretty good, but he'd been too engrossed in football at the time to get fired up over anything else. In fact, he'd never gotten into science fiction.

Over the years he'd been a big reader of fiction and biographies, but to him any talk about aliens coming to Earth was absurd. So far no one had produced an alien body except in the film *E.T.* He'd never seen a crop circle, a vampire, a shape-shifter or a ghost. If he couldn't see it and feel it, he didn't believe it. Chaz needed proof.

He moved on to the preface where she'd defined terms. A stargrazer was a meteor. During a meteor shower, some swept close enough to Earth to be caught in its gravity. The meteor in her novel came from the constellation Perseus. She spent a page describing the constellation and the stars within it.

Somehow Chaz hadn't expected to be captivated by the book's preface and certainly not this fast. As he started to scroll further, his radio came on too loud, jarring him from his thoughts. It was time to listen to her show.

The tail end of the news was followed by a lead-in of an ancient-sounding instrument from Nepal or some-place, blaring a cavernously deep single note. It grew louder until he felt his body vibrating with it. Chaz didn't like the sensation. He set the reader aside and turned down the volume.

The announcer started speaking. "If you've been jolted out of your comfort zone, that means it's the twenty-first hour and you've just tuned in to the nation-ally syndicated *Stargrazer Paranormal Show* on your AM 500 radio dial. This is coming from the Ionosphere Network, high atop its signal tower in the Wasatch Mountains above Salt Lake City, Utah, broadcasting to two hundred and fifteen affiliates throughout the United States and Canada."

His dark brows lifted. That was a lot of radio sta-tions. He couldn't believe how many people listened to a show like this. Barry Winslow had pulled off a coup being able to produce Lacey Pomeroy's program in Salt Lake. She obviously loved what she did or she wouldn't have gotten back into it after leaving California.

"If you're easily terrified or suffer from heart trouble, we advise that you immediately turn off your radio since we will not be held responsible."

A chuckle escaped Chaz's throat.

"The next three exploratory hours are only for the inquisitive, unafraid mind open to all the possibilities in an unending number of universes expanding as we speak. Here is your host and founder of the program, Lacey Pomeroy."

"Happy summer solstice, everybody. This is our June 20 show, the one we've all been waiting for, and you know why. On this Thursday night, the earth's axial tilt is most inclined toward the sun and is celebrated from culture to culture within our galaxy by gatherings and rituals. And *visitors....*"

Chaz blinked in surprise to hear the mellow feminine voice that came out over the airwaves. Besides having a lilt that was easy on the ear, it was sexy, but not in a way that was put on or unnatural. By her opening words, you would never know she was being terrorized.

"The boards are already lighting up from Florida to Canada. I'm going to take our first call from Max, who's been waiting the longest. He's in the Hole-in-the-Rock area of southern Utah, a very beautiful and mysterious place full of ancient lore. You're on the air, Max."

"Hi, Lacey. Yours is my favorite show. I listen to you all the time."

"Thank you. That's music to my ears. What's going on down there?"

"Plenty. I've been four-wheeling around here with my buddies in a group we call the Wolf Pack. There are eight Jeeps in the group. We've all got our headlights shining on this huge wall of petroglyphs that are three thousand years old. These aren't painted. They've been chiseled into the rock. The images are incredible. If you saw them, you would *know* the people who did this art-work are from another world."

"Describe some for our audience."

"One type of creature is represented more than the others. It's like a rounded rectangle with an oblong head. The antennae curl around the sides, but it's not like any animal you've ever seen. There are triangle shapes set at random and mysterious symbols like a corkscrew amidst dozens of suns. These people wor-shipped the sun, which is a source of their energy. We're thinking tonight we'll see one of their triangles land."

"It wouldn't surprise me, Max. A report just came in of a triangular-shaped UFO sighting over a park in Chongqing, China. And a few days ago Japan's first lady claimed to have flown on an alien spaceship that she said was triangular shaped and took her to Venus while she slept." Chaz shook his head, totally amused.

"I guess you couldn't get an interview with her for your show."

"I'm afraid not, but I tell you what. If you have con-tact tonight, call in to the station tomorrow night and we'll feature you as a guest. Now we're moving on to our next caller from Rapid City, South Dakota. You're on the air."

"Hi, Lacey. It's Mel on the Harley. Remember me?"

"The Sturgis guy?"

"Yeah. Damn, you're good. Me and the gang are hanging out in the Badlands tonight. There's a ton of meteor rocks out here. We figure we're going to see a shower of them before the night's over and who knows what else. We were wondering if any of your listeners have been out here and have seen anything else unusual. I'll hang up and listen."

"You all heard Mel. If you've had an out-of-this-world experience in the Badlands, I'll ask Stewart, who's working the phones, to fit you into the call lineup. We're moving on to Moline, Illinois. Am I speaking to Roseanne?"

"Yes. Hi! I'm so excited to be on your show. I've tried for two months to get on and now I'm so nervous I'm scared."

"Hey—we're all friends. How old are you?"

"Fifteen. I've never talked to a real-live author before. I read your Stargrazer book and loved it so much I wondered if you'd autograph it for me."

"Sure. Send it in care of the show. Off the air Stewart will give you the P.O. address."

"Thanks so much. Oh, before I hang up, I was just wondering if you're going to write another Stargrazer story. You could do one where a guy from Algol lands in the Badlands by accident. That would be so cool, especially if you made him as gorgeous as Percy, maybe his cousin? I'm the president of your fan club. I set up a Twitter account and a Facebook page dedicated to you. Our club has over twelve hundred members and we want you to write another book."

"That's very flattering, Roseanne. Maybe one day when I have more time."

"Please make it soon—we can't wait!"

Chaz had already heard enough to be curious about her novel. Twelve hundred teens waiting for another book? And that was just in one fan club. How come Lacey Garvey Pomeroy hadn't written more than one?

He was anxious to get started reading the story, but she'd come back on the air after an ad and was talking to a new caller. Chaz needed to listen to the whole program. Undoubtedly her stalker was tuned in, picking up on her every word, and might even be one of the callers.

Much to his surprise, as he listened for the next two and a half hours, jotting down notes, he didn't suffer a moment's boredom except for the ads and station breaks. She ended her show with the announcement about playing a tape from last year's Summer Solstice Conference in Milwaukee tomorrow night.

"When I open the program, I'll let you know the exact time it will come on so none of you will miss it. I've had so many calls about it, I decided tomorrow night would be the perfect time to air it again. That's all from the Ionosphere for tonight."

Because the two phoned death threats had come around the same time as the summer solstice, Chaz made a note to find out more about this conference. He wondered if the note placed on her car had also happened around June 20 of last year. There might be a connection.

Mrs. Pomeroy had followed the instructions he'd given her to the letter, and she'd done it brilliantly. Wide awake now, he turned off the radio and started reading the novel's prologue.

Apparently a time traveler from the variable planet Algol located in the Perseus constellation had flown to Earth on a stargrazer. His name was Percy, a brooding, unhappy soul who once a year rode the meteor shower, roving from one parallel universe to another. He'd been to thousands of them, but never bonded with one spot.

He had no age. He had friends, but life had made him a loner—his family had been killed aeons ago when he was a child. He was looking for something he couldn't find, but was positive he would know it if he ever came upon it.

Chaz closed his eyes for a minute, surprised by what he'd just read. It was as if the author had described Chaz's life down to certain unknown details about him. Ridiculous as it was, he felt bemused by this piece of fantasy fiction where his own life seemed to have been exposed.

He also had to admit to being fascinated and continued to read about Percy, who'd been told to bypass Earth because it could be dangerous for him, but he went anyway because it was his nature to take risks.

The author had nailed that trait in Chaz, too. He got off the bed and grabbed for the last piece of licorice on the side table. A little sugar heightened his enjoyment as he walked around the room reading the description of Percy.

Lacey Pomeroy might have been a teenager when she'd written this book, but her insights gave him the impression she'd been going on a hundred at the time. Where had a brain like hers come from? The same place as Heinlein's, Chaz supposed.

Chuckling to himself, he took a shower and got ready for bed. He needed sleep and would finish reading in the morning. But when he eventually climbed under the covers, he realized he was as hooked by Lacey Pomeroy's writing as Roseanne, the girl who'd called into the show wanting the author to pen another novel.

He reached for the reader, promising himself he would read only a little more. For a teen, Lacey had possessed an amazing imagination. Percy always arrived in another universe by a meteor depositing him over a body of water. When he landed on Earth, he found himself in Hudson Bay near the New York City docks. Luckily, his skills included underwater prowess.

Riveted by her tale, Chaz wondered if he'd find more of himself in the character she'd created and scrolled down to begin chapter one. But realizing he needed sleep, he forced himself to turn off the reader. He was supposed to be using this research to help him get a handle on Lacey Pomeroy's case, not focusing on himself.

He really was messed up. If the other P.I.'s in the office, particularly his buds Mitch and Travis, knew about his interest in a teenage sci-fi novel, they'd laugh themselves sick.

What wasn't laughable was that someone in Salt Lake or California was after this woman. Even if those phone calls had been a couple of malicious pranks with nothing more sinister intended, it still meant this person had found Lacey's unlisted number and had invaded her privacy. The culprit needed to be arrested. Let a judge slap on a harsh fine and order them into counseling to be watched.

But if they were clinically delusional, waiting to do exactly what had been put in the death threats, then they needed to be stopped yesterday.

Both phone threats and the note on her car appeared to have been tied to her work with the paranormal. But that might have been a deliberate ploy by the perpetrator to throw any police investigation off the scent. Chaz didn't know yet.

One thing he'd learned so far. What he'd heard and read tonight could spark irrational jealousy in someone who wished they'd written a novel twelve hundred teenagers were clamoring to read, but had been rejected by a slew of publishers. Or had been up for the Nebula Award and had lost out.

Certainly someone who wanted to be a famous radio or TV personality with a particular slant like Mrs. Pomeroy's and couldn't make it to first base could be consumed by envy that had escalated beyond normal bounds. Or maybe it was someone who *had* achieved great success, but it still wasn't enough.

Professional jealousy abounded in the workplace. Plenty of homicides every year attested to that. He recalled hearing about the deliberate injury to a beautiful, talented Olympic ice skater by another competitor. It had been ugly.

But this case was uglier. Or would be if the stalker followed through on his or her threats.

Doing his homework tonight had given Chaz a place to start, but as they'd announced at the beginning of her show, this was only one possibility in an unending number of expanding universes.

Chapter Two

The radio station was one of many businesses in a strip mall located in the Fort Union business area of Salt Lake. It wasn't far from the Parkridge condo complex where Lacey lived. On Friday night, after putting her precious Abby to bed with lots of stories and kisses, she thanked her sister and left. At eight-thirty it was still twilight as she backed her blue Passat out of her garage and drove the short distance to work.

She found it a strange experience knowing she was probably being watched by her stalker along with a crew of people working for the P.I. firm. Everyone in her line of vision or behind her was suspect. At the moment her life felt surreal.

Apparently Barry had okayed the work order for the satellite-dish people to come in and check the equipment for problems. That way Stewart wouldn't question letting them in.

Lacey couldn't imagine the security guard, Ben, a retired policeman and grandfather, or Stewart, the intern who was engaged to be married and in his last year of college, had anything to do with this. But she'd read enough mysteries and watched enough police shows to know anything was possible.

Hadn't she said it on her show? Anything *was* possible and she had to believe it.

She normally dressed in casual tops and jeans for comfort, but for work she always wore a dressier top and sandals to look more professional around the staff, radio hosts and guests who came in and out. For tonight she'd put on a summery print blouse in earth tones with a flutter sleeve.

Stewart's office was on the other side of the glass partition so they could always have eye contact and use hand signals when necessary. He stuck up notes, letting her know the name and location of the caller waiting on the line.

Most of the time they had fun smiling and reacting to the different callers. There were the talkers who wouldn't stop, the ones who couldn't talk once they got on the air, the cynics, the gushy ones, the ones who flirted, the ones who wanted her to endorse their Area 51 and Bermuda Triangle websites.

Sometimes a psychic called in giving her information about her future. On certain nights a ghost-watcher group called in from a cemetery to let the audience hear a child's cry. A certain Wicca liked to talk about the wheel of life. Another called from the edge of a hole in the ground that had no bottom. The calls ran the gamut and she loved it.

But the calls on her own phones had caused her to wonder. Maybe Stewart *was* her stalker. He had access to both her phone numbers and wanted to become a radio personality. No longer could she look at him the same way.

Her fear for Abby's and her family's safety dominated her every breath and thought. There was a definite risk in exposing herself to the public over the air. Say what you will, it invited this kind of evil and now her entire family was threatened.

She knew Barry was doing everything possible to help her through this because he didn't want her to quit. He was the one person she didn't suspect, not when he'd hired a P.I. at the network's expense to catch this demon. Her biggest fault was agreeing to keep the show going after she'd come back to Salt Lake.

That death threat on her windshield should have been enough of a retardant. Regardless of the growing ratings and increased salary, no career was worth this kind of horror.

Lacey had enough savings to fly her and her family to another part of the country where they could live for a month away from the spotlight with different names. If this lunatic wasn't caught by the time they returned to Salt Lake, she would ask the P.I. how to go about hiring some good bodyguards.

She turned into the broad alley behind the strip mall. It was a busy weekend night. Other cars were going in and out to movies and restaurants. She drove halfway down to park in the well-lit area at the back door of the station. Her program followed the *Smart Finance Show* with Kurt Smart. His black Audi was parked next to Stewart's white Nissan.

Stewart usually came in early to handle the business end and collect all the faxes for her show. The most interesting or relevant were earmarked for her attention. She would glance through them during the ads to see if she could use any of them. Tonight the thought of getting a fax from the stalker almost immobilized her, but she had to get out of her car and go inside.

After she'd let herself in the back door with the remote, she hurried down the hall to her office on the other side of Stewart's. She poked her head inside to let him know she'd arrived.

He glanced up with a smile. Kurt was still on the air.

"How are things going?"

"Busy. I went through your faxes. You got a ton and will never get through them tonight."

"What else is new?" she teased, forcing herself to act as if nothing was wrong. The fact that he didn't alert her to a disturbing one caused her to let out the breath she'd been holding.

But then he wouldn't have said anything if he were the culprit. Or maybe he would have....

Fear was driving her crazy.

"Barry said some guys from a dish-network crew are coming in sometime tonight to check out the equipment. Apparently it's the only time they can come and Barry wants the work done no matter what, so he says just ignore them."

"Oh. Okay. By the way, I want to play the Summer Solstice Conference tape from last year at ten."

"Right. Barry mentioned it. I have it lined up."

Unable to concentrate on anything, she picked up the receiver of the station phone to call her sister and make sure everything was all right at the condo with Abby. But then she thought better of it. Before long it was nine o'clock and time for the news before her segment started. She grabbed the faxes and left her office.

"Hey, Lacey—" Kurt was just coming out of the booth. "You're looking beautiful as usual." He always said something nice. *Everyone is suspect. Even Kurt.*

"Thanks. How did your show go tonight?"

"Callers are grumbling about the bad economy."

"It is pretty bad."

"Yup. Well, have a good one," he murmured before heading toward the back door.

She slipped inside the broadcast booth and set the faxes on the desk. After sitting down, she put on her earphones, adjusted the mic and gave Stewart the nod that she was ready. It terrified her to think that the stalker might be listening tonight, planning when he was going to kill her and her daughter.

Lacey had never had ulcers, but knew she was getting one. Whenever she thought of anything happening to Abby, the pain hit her like someone was torching her insides with a soldering gun. The antacids she'd been taking all day hadn't helped.

She waited for the long lead-in to end, then launched into the program, reminding the listeners that highlights from the Summer Solstice Conference would be aired at ten o'clock. Lacey was counting the seconds until she could talk to the P.I.

Who knew how good he was. Someone with a background in law enforcement didn't necessarily have the ability to solve a case like this. Lacey didn't know the odds when it came to stalking cases, but feared they were against her.

Barry seemed to have faith in this agency, but he was desperate to keep her on the air. Little did he know she was desperate enough to leave Salt Lake with her loved ones to keep everyone safe.

By the time ten o'clock rolled around, she was so anxious to meet the P.I., she'd developed a headache. Until now she and her mom had been running on their faith in Barry's judgment, but that might not be enough.

The advertisements ended and Stewart started the tape. That was her cue to look through the faxes and pretend she was busy. In a minute she heard the door open. Out of the periphery she saw a man enter the booth wearing a light blue uniform.

His powerful body moved around the enclosed space checking various pieces of electronic equipment, then he came near her and hunkered down while ostensibly checking the floor plugs. Not all people smelled good up close, but he did. Suddenly he lifted his head.

Although she was quite sure she'd never before seen this man, there was something about him that was strangely familiar. He had black hair that was long enough to curl at his neck and was very tall—maybe around six foot three. He was broad-shouldered, well-cut and lean, with strong, unerring hands. But there was something about his eyes.... Something that reminded her of...Percy!

Strange how in this circumstance, life imitated art instead of the other way around. The character in her novel had such eyes. A mixture of green and yellow.

Years earlier, after she'd seen a shooting star, she'd created a guy in her mind. He'd possessed unusual qualities and traits because he'd come from another universe. The meteor he was on had flown too close to Earth and had been caught in its gravitational pull.

Seeing the eyes she'd imagined years before in the flesh was a visceral experience for her.

CHAZ'S BREATH CAUGHT. THE fantastic-looking woman with honey-red hair bouncing on her shoulders was staring at him with the most amazing smoky-blue eyes. In that fluttery blouse and jeans she filled out to perfection, there wasn't a man alive who wouldn't follow her down the street just to get a better look at her.

Barry Winslow had filled him in on the basics about her. Her husband had been killed while he was in the Coast Guard and she'd moved back to Salt Lake from Long Beach. She'd been a widow for a year and had a three-year-old daughter. The producer didn't know if she had a boyfriend or a lover. He'd never seen her with one or heard her talk about one.

That didn't mean a stream of men hadn't tried to get to first base with her. If one of them couldn't take rejection, he might be her stalker.

He murmured softly, "Dr. Livingston, I presume."

His first words erased her startled expression. A tiny, unexpected smile broke one corner of her mouth. He saw pure intelligence flow from those dark-fringed eyes before she said, "I heard rumors you were coming, Mr. Stanley."

Despite the deadly seriousness of the situation, he felt this palpitating connection to her. *An out-of-body experience?* That was the only way to describe it.

"One of the crew is up on the roof checking out the dish while he's videotaping the area. I'll be leaving when he comes back down. That only gives us a few minutes to talk. I know you have a lot of questions, but save them until we meet tomorrow. What's your normal schedule like in the morning?"

She kept going through the faxes on her desk, pretending to read them. "Now that it's summer, my mother usually comes over on Saturday and we take my daughter to the park. Afterward we go grocery shopping and have lunch someplace before we go back for Abby's nap."

"Do you usually go to the same store?"

"Yes."

"Then I'll call your mother and tell her my plan. Give me the name and address of the store."

When she told him, he said, "Your mother will drive tomorrow and take you to the grocery store at eleven. While she does some shopping with your daughter, you'll walk through to Produce and tell them you need to pick up a salad in the back room. I'll be there to let you out the rear door. We'll drive to my office to discuss your case. Did you keep the death threat on the voice mail of your cell phone?"

"Yes. I saved it for evidence. The death threat on my landline is still recorded, too."

"Good. Here's the plan. When we're through talking at my office tomorrow, you'll call your mother on the new phone I'm going to give you. She'll have your new number and know it's you. Once you've told her you'll meet her back at the grocery store, I'll take you there so you can enter through the produce department door. Okay?"

"Yes."

"A couple more things. When was the last time you went to your mailbox?"

"Two days ago. I've been afraid to get it."

"Where is your box located?"

"In a row of boxes between my building and the one next door."

"On your way out to your mother's car, I want you to collect the mail and put it in your purse. We'll go through it at my office. I'd also like the most recent photos of your immediate and extended family for me to make copies of and distribute to my crew. Bring a wedding album and guest book if you have them for identification purposes."

"I'll do it."

"Good. Now I've got to go."

Her eyes grew suspiciously bright. "Thank you, Mr. Roylance."

"Call me Chaz." Reading her mind, he said, "It's short for Charles. I always disliked my given name."

CHAZ LET HIMSELF OUT, NODDING to the radio intern manning the phones. The night watchman opened the main door for him. He walked over to a big van with a dish on the top and climbed in.

The van was one of the firm's many electronic-surveillance vehicles set up with state-of-the-art equipment. Adam was driving. An unmarried demolitions and electronics expert, Adam was home from the Middle East after deployment. He'd applied for a job with Roman, who was training him to become a P.I. Adam had uncanny instincts that had prompted Chaz to put him on the case.

They passed a janitorial-service truck parked a few cars away where Lon, a retired police officer who'd headed several SWAT teams in his time, was on duty for Chaz. He'd be tailing Lacey Pomeroy until six in the morning, when another member of the crew took over.

"Let's head over to Walmart." Adam nodded. "What kind of traffic did you see out here tonight?"

"A lot of vehicles, some foot."

"Good. We'll analyze the tape when I meet you at the office tomorrow."

He nodded again. "What's she like?"

Lacey Pomeroy kept on surprising him in stunning ways. Tonight it was her incredible looks *and* her sophistication. Disinclined to talk about her while he was trying to sort out all his feelings, he said, "She's handling this well."

He didn't tell Adam how she'd held herself rigid and took shallow breaths, or how her fingers tortured the top fax. He definitely didn't tell him about the voluptuous line of her mouth when she'd let go with that little unexpected smile, or her delicious fragrance that reminded him of strawberries.

Some people chattered away when they were frightened. She'd done just the opposite, displaying admirable poise under precarious circumstances. Where did hair like that come from? Red shot with gold, or gold shot with red… He'd never seen color and texture so tantalizing. He'd wanted to lift the strands to the light and play with them.

"We've arrived."

Adam's voice jerked him back to the present. "Thanks. See you tomorrow." Chaz got out of the van and walked over to his Forerunner parked in the lot full of late-night shoppers. He drove straight back to his condo. Now that he'd met the unforgettable author of *The Stargrazer from Algol,* he was more eager than ever to get into the body of the book.

After he got ready for bed, he climbed in and reached for the reader, intrigued to see how she'd started chapter one to capture the mind of a teen, her target audience.

Percy was lounging on the deck of an ocean liner observing the earthlings when he spotted a family walking his way. As they moved past him, his eyes connected with the blue gaze of one of the daughters and there was a sudden spike in his body temperature. The ferocity of it left him feeling so physically ill, he could hardly find the strength to move.

LACEY HAD GIVEN ABBY A cherry Ring Pop to lick while she pushed the shopping cart along the fruit aisle. When they reached the area near the back of the store, she whispered to her mother, "I'll call you."

Quickly, before Abby caught on, Lacey headed for the doorway leading to the area where produce was unloaded from trucks. Aware the stalker could be watching, she had to appear natural as she walked through. Two employees in back were cutting up vegetables and fruits in a room filled with crates. They nodded to her, but her gaze was drawn to the tall, striking man holding the outer door open.

Dressed in a short-sleeved black crewneck with boot-cut jeans, Chaz Roylance filled her vision. She hurried toward him. His gaze swept over her, and despite her anxiety, Lacey felt her pulse race. When she'd told her friend Brenda that no man would ever interest her again after Ted, she hadn't met Chaz Roylance. "Climb in the green Forerunner parked outside."

She did his bidding and fastened the seat belt. Within seconds he joined her and drove them past the rear of the supermarket and out to another street away from the store parking area. At the first stoplight he glanced at her. Though his eyes reflected male interest, he was a total professional. "You were right on time, Mrs. Pomeroy. That makes my plans easier to carry out."

"If you only knew how grateful I am…"

"I'm happy to help. Do you mind if I call you Lacey?"

"No."

"Just so you know, I'm wearing a mini tape recorder to pick up our conversation. Is that all right with you?"

"Yes." The man was trying to help her. How could she possibly object, especially when he was up front about it?

The light changed and they took off toward Wasatch Boulevard, where her mother had told her he worked. "I have a confession to make right off the bat."

She stared blindly out the window, wishing she weren't so physically aware of him. "What's that?"

"I've never believed in aliens or the paranormal, but if anything could make me reconsider, it would be your radio show."

Surprised, she turned to him. "You listened?"

He nodded. "To all of Thursday night's program. I've also read your book to the part where Percy sees the earthling and his temperature spikes to one hundred and twenty degrees like a hot plume of gas from Algol's something region."

Lacey smiled, secretly delighted by the admission that he'd gone to that much trouble to learn about her. "Hebulon."

His lips twitched, making him even more attractive. "That's it. I'm supposing that your traveler has to find a place to hide so the platinum streaks in his hair don't turn silver in front of the passengers. I confess I can't wait to find out."

She chuckled.

"It's no wonder your fifteen-year-old listener Rose-anne and her army of twelve hundred are waiting for another story."

An *army?* Lacey's chuckle turned into quiet laughter.

"From what I've researched, you've only had one novel published, unless you're published under a pseudonym or two."

"No. There's only the one book."

"How come? You can't tell me you don't have dozens more in your computer files. I imagine your publisher would steal them if it were possible."

"That's very flattering." She recrossed her legs. "I do have other novels, but none of them are finished."

"Why not?"

"Because I went to Stanford in California and started writing a column for the *Stanford Daily*. Between studying for classes in my geophysics major, keeping up with the deadlines and doing a weekly paranormal segment at the university's radio station, I had to put my novel writing aside."

"I can't imagine why," he teased.

She laughed.

"And after college, you went into radio instead of pursuing a career in geophysics. What happened?"

"I was torn. I loved science and writing, but it was very flattering to be given an opportunity to do a paranormal show when it was offered to me. To be honest, I didn't see how it would catch on, and after a couple of weeks I was sure it would fail. When it didn't, I only expected it to last for a season because I'm a writer first and foremost. But my old boss kept pressing me to stay another season.

"My future dream is to write science fiction for adults using the knowledge from my geophysics background. Those stories will be more advanced and interest people of all ages. As for the young-adult stories, one day I'll finish the ones I started."

He darted her a puzzled glance. "Tell me something, with all this going on in that mind of yours, how did you manage to fit in a wedding?"

"It wasn't easy with Ted being in the Coast Guard."

"Where did you two meet?"

Lacey had to remember he was firing all these questions at her because he was investigating her case, not because he was interested in her. She realized that everything she told him could be critical to finding the stalker. To hold back any information would only hurt her. But she couldn't help but wonder what it would be like to have met him naturally. Would he still have found her interesting?

"There'd been a UFO sighting over the Bay Area. I'd been working a program segment for the radio and went to Fisherman's Wharf to interview people who'd seen it and tape their responses. Ted happened to be there with some of his buddies on weekend leave from Long Beach. We started talking and one thing led to another. We got married six months later, as soon as I graduated. He's been gone a year."

She heard him exhale. "I'm sorry for your loss. You have my deepest sympathy. Ten years ago my wife's death hit me hard. She died from cervical cancer and it took me a long time to recover."

Lacey bit her lip. "I'm so sorry for you, too. Do you have children?"

"No."

The P.I. had to be in his mid-thirties by now. "I have my Abby. Without her, I don't know what I'd do." How sad for him not to have had a child. How hard. "If this stalker tries to hurt her…" She clutched her purse, unable to go on talking.

"Take heart, Lacey. I plan to catch this person before anything happens. When I do, your case will be handed over to the police and they'll make an arrest."

Since Chaz had acted so fast, plus gone to the trouble of listening to her show and reading her book, his vow convinced her he would do whatever was humanly possible to help her. No wonder her mother had felt encouraged. He did instill confidence. "I believe you," she said in a trembly voice.

He turned off the highway and pulled around the back of his office. After shutting off the engine he eyed her frankly. "In a case like this, to have trust between the two of us means everything. We're off to a good start. Let's go inside where we'll lay out a plan."

The Lufka P.I. Agency looked like any well-managed business office, with a dozen or so people on the premises. Chaz ushered her into his private office, supplying coffee for both of them. The attractive owner, Roman Lufka, came in and introduced himself. Apparently he was the one who'd listened to Barry's phone call. After he went out again, Chaz asked to see her mail.

She opened her purse. Aside from the ads and brochures, she had only three bills and what looked like a wedding invitation.

"May I open them?"

"Of course."

He did a quick check of the bills, then the larger envelope before darting her a glance. "This is an invitation to visit some time-share rentals in Park City. Free knives are being given for taking a tour."

"Just what I wanted," she said with a haunted whisper as he handed everything back to her.

"Do you know anyone at this business? Have they been a sponsor of your show?"

"No, but I'm aware they've been around for several years."

He put the mail aside. "Check your mailbox every day, but don't open anything until I'm with you. Now, let me see your cell phone."

She handed it to him and put the mail back in her purse. "There are four messages to listen to."

He put on the speakerphone and played the first one.

I can hardly wait to see your blood on my hands, you bitch. So watch out and keep looking over your shoulder, because I'm right behind you and plan to cut out your freakin' heart first. Then I'll start on your daughter.... Both will be an in-the-body experience you won't forget.

His eyes flicked to hers. "Did the message on your landline sound the same? I'm not talking words."

"I know what you mean. Yes, it was the same man's voice."

"Do you remember the essence of that message?"

"It said something about my next experience burning up my brain, literally."

He cocked his dark head. "Mr. Winslow told me about the note you found on your car windshield a year ago outside the funeral home. Try to remember any details of what it said."

Lacey shivered. "I should have saved it for evidence, but at the time I was in so much pain over Ted, I threw it away. It talked about aliens killing my husband and now they were going to burn up my daughter and me, part by part. Something like that," she murmured.

"Was the note pieced together with words from magazine cutouts? Handwritten?"

"Neither. It was typed on a piece of paper."

"What about grammar and spelling?"

She blinked. "Nothing stands out in my mind, but I think it was all in caps."

He nodded. "Let's trace the call on this phone and see where it leads."

She waited while he pressed the digits, then he was talking to someone. After a few minutes he hung up. "That call was placed from a phone booth in the E.R. waiting room of a hospital in Denver, Colorado. Anyone could have called."

Lacey couldn't prevent the shudder that attacked her body.

"I'll be interested to see where the call on your landline came from." A sober expression broke out on his rugged features. "We don't know yet if the caller is the same person who left the note under your windshield wiper, but we do know two important things. One, it's a human, not an alien entity harassing you.

"Two, whoever phoned you was using a twenty-dollar voice converter that's placed over a regular phone or a cell to distort the sound. They're so small they can be worn on a key chain. It means your stalker could be a man or a woman."

Chapter Three

Lacey's quiet gasp told Chaz a lot. "The possibility that it might be a woman never occurred to you?"

"Not really," she murmured. "I usually think of a woman harassing an ex-spouse or ex-boyfriend."

"Would it interest you to know that thirteen percent of all stalking cases are committed by women, and forty-eight percent of them stalk other women?"

"You mean they harass their ex-partners of the same gender because they're no longer together?"

"In some cases. But in others there's been no sexual intimacy. It has more to do with anger and hostility often stemming from an actual or perceived rejection by the victim."

Lacey shook her head. "I've never given any of this much thought before."

"Most people don't have to. One of the reasons you haven't is because the available evidence on women stalkers hasn't been afforded the degree of seriousness attached to male stalkers. Eighty-four percent of men stalk a female victim, so it's in the news more. Keep in mind that just because we don't hear about it as often doesn't mean women are any less intrusive or persistent in their stalking, or pose any less of a threat to their victims, physical or otherwise."

Just remembering what had happened in South America proved to Chaz that women trained by the enemy were just as capable of violence as men.

He saw her flinch. "It's all horrifying."

"I agree. But I want to assure you that most stalkers are not psychotic. In general, they suffer from depression and substance abuse, or a personality disorder. Female stalkers are significantly less likely than males to have a history of criminal or violent criminal offenses.

"What we'll do is make a list of men and women who've been close to you in the past or who are close to you now. Perhaps none of them are involved, but it's not as common for a person you've never known to harass you. That narrows the field a great deal and you should be confident that we'll find your stalker soon."

Chaz had given her a lot to think about, but he'd only scratched the surface. "First, I want to know about your daily schedule apart from your work," he said.

"Basically I take care of my daughter until I go to work Monday through Friday. We play and go to the park, shop, eat out, drop by her nana's. While she naps, I work on my material for the radio program and take care of correspondence. Sometimes on weekends we get together with my aunt's family or I meet a friend for lunch, but generally speaking it's the same schedule."

"Tell me about your immediate family."

"That would be Mom and Ruth."

"Does your mother work?"

"Yes. She's a math whiz and teaches part-time in

the math department at the University of Utah. That's where she met my dad, who was a bioengineer and worked for a company developing new software for the medical field."

He smiled. "Your smarts come from great genes."

"My parents were brilliant. When she got pregnant with me, Mom stayed at home, and didn't go back to teaching until after Ruth went into junior high. By then I'd started high school. We're two years apart.

"After I moved home from California Mom wanted to help me, so she cut down her teaching load to only two days a week. She doesn't have to work. Dad left her well enough off, but she likes to keep busy. She's also involved in her church group and spends time with her sister, my aunt Mary, and her family who live in North Salt Lake."

"Is Ruth equally gifted?"

"Mom once told me Ruth had a higher IQ than anyone in our family."

"What kind of work does she do?"

"After high school graduation she took different jobs until the one at the cell-phone store. It paid her a salary plus commission. She saved enough money there to pay for flying lessons."

"That's interesting."

"I know. It was a surprise to Mom and me, but she can be moody at times, so you never know what she'll decide to do next. Once she'd obtained her license, she worked several places and ended up flying for an air cargo company in Idaho Falls. But then the bad economy impacted everything. A month ago she was let go."

Or maybe Lacey's sister couldn't get along with

people at that job, either. But Chaz kept his thoughts to himself.

"What's Ruth doing now?"

"She's living with our mother, trying to find work. Mom's been helping her out financially. I am, too, in my own way. Since I always need a babysitter at night, I asked her if she'd like to tend Abby for me and I'd pay her until she found a new job. She took me up on the offer, for which I'm grateful."

"What about her social life?"

"Ruth's very good-looking and has always had a ton of boyfriends, but from what I can tell, those relationships are stormy. Since she's been home I've heard her on the phone with a guy named Bruce. I don't know if it's very serious. One day she'll probably get married to someone I've never heard of, then spring him on the family. It would be just like her."

"Your sister sounds like her own person," he murmured. He'd be interested to know why exactly she'd been let go from her pilot's job.

"She's that and more. I love her."

"That's nice. I never had a sibling." He studied her for a minute. "Who babysat for you before?"

"Julie Howard. I've known her for a long time. Her family lives across the street from my mother. She's college-age and attends the university. Mom heard she wanted part-time work. The hours I could offer were perfect for her."

Chaz would check out the babysitter later. "The questions I'm going to ask you now will make you uncomfortable, but if I'm to help you, I need to know the truth."

He noticed she swallowed hard. "I understand that."

"How many intimate relationships did you have before your husband? I'm talking going to bed together."

Lacey squirmed in the chair. "Your warning didn't help me," she whispered. "Since a stalker is threatening me, I guess I have to answer that question." She lowered her head. "Much as I'd like to tell you it's none of your business, I can't do that, not when my life and Abby's are on the line. The truth is, I didn't have any intimate relationships before Ted."

Chaz believed her. In this day and age, that was quite a statement to make. "And since?"

Again she stirred restlessly. He could see how hard this was for her. Hell, he wouldn't like this kind of inquisition, either.

"There's been no one."

"Tell me about the men who wanted to take you out. Were there a lot of those?"

She smoothed the hair away from her forehead. "I dated some in high school and college when I had the time. I made out with some of them, but I was never in love and the chemistry wasn't right for me to want to sleep with any of them."

Maybe not, but that couldn't be said for the men who would have had an immediate crush on her and that crush could have turned into an obsession. "Was there one guy who wouldn't give up?"

"Yes." A quick smile came and went. "It was Ted, but then I didn't want him to give up. It was one of those situations where I let him chase me until I caught him."

He chuckled. "How long were you married?"

"Two and a half years."

"May I see a picture of him?"

She opened her wallet and handed him one of Ted in his Coast Guard uniform. A nice-looking guy with dark blond hair. What a tragedy she'd lost him. He gave the picture back.

"Do you have a romantic interest in your life right now?"

"No. I couldn't imagine it."

He'd gone through that stage after losing his wife. "When did your husband die?"

"June 18. I was supposed to have flown out for the summer solstice convention in Milwaukee. I'd only planned to be gone two days. My mother was going to fly down to Long Beach to tend Abby while I was gone and stay for the rest of the week. But my whole world fell apart when the Coast Guard informed me Ted had been killed. You more than anyone would understand what that moment was like."

"I'm afraid I do."

It was possible Chaz's theory about the note and phone calls being connected to the summer solstice convention had substance. Or it could be more directly related to Ted. The note had showed up a year ago at Ted's funeral. One year later on the first anniversary of his death, she'd received two phone threats. If the stalker wanted Lacey's exclusive attention and had felt rejected by her, then he or she was glad Ted Pomeroy was out of the way, thus removing the biggest obstacle.

Then again, the culprit might be motivated by professional jealousy and would do everything possible to scare Lacey off the air permanently. Including her daughter, Abby, in the threats would rachet up the fear factor.

"Do you normally meet friends at a convention like that, or are the attendees strangers?"

"A bit of both. I belong to a core group of dedicated paranormal enthusiasts, but meet new people at each conference. They're as fascinated by the unexplainable as I am. We discuss the latest findings and compare notes. I gather information for my radio show. One of them, Gil Lawrence, who's a journalist, made certain I was sent the tape from the Milwaukee convention."

"Where does this special group come from?"

"All over the country."

"How long have you known this group?"

"About six years. After I graduated from Stanford, I attended a paranormal conference in Seattle and we became friends practically overnight because of our mutual interest."

"Are these people prominent?"

"They're a unique bunch of scientists, pilots, government workers, intellectuals, writers and journalists who've lost some credibility at their places of work because they profess to believe in paranormal activity."

He could understand that. "How do you stay in touch with them?"

"Mostly by email, but when there's some really exciting news, we phone."

"Do these people have both of your phone numbers?"

Her eyes darkened with emotion. "Yes. And my address."

"Are you a large group?"

"No. There are twelve right now. We try to meet at a conference every other month. For the most part, we've been able to keep it up."

"Are these people married? Single?"

"Both."

Chaz reached for her phone and turned on the speaker so they could listen to the other messages she hadn't erased. He let them play, then asked, "Who's Dave?"

"The man returning my call is Dave Lignel, one of the long-standing group members who's married and has a family. He's a commercial-airline pilot who at the moment is keeping me apprised on some lights in the night sky neither he nor his copilot could identify on his last flight to South America."

Just hearing the name South America filled his mind with images of what had happened there…images he fought to forget.

"That woman who informed me about the book on Sasquatch? She works in the circulation department at the main library. As you heard, the third call was from my dentist's office reminding me of my next checkup."

Chaz got up to turn on the television and play the tapes Adam and the other crew people had brought in this morning. "I want you to watch these surveillance videos filming outside your condo and the radio station. If you see something that alarms you, I need to know."

As she identified neighbors going in and out of her condo building, he took notes. "We all pretty much leave each other alone, but everyone in my building is friendly. The couple below me has two children, so we have more in common and chat now and then."

"How about the people at the radio station?"

She pointed out one of the daytime talk show hosts who'd gone inside the radio station during her program, but hadn't stayed long. "That's Sally who does the *Tiptoe Through the Tulips* garden show on Saturdays.

She's in her sixties and gives gardening classes at the water conservancy park. There could be any number of reasons why she dropped by there last night.

"The other guy just going in the station is Greg Stevens. He does the *Sports and Celebrities* midnight show. It lasts till four in the morning when the local newscaster Adrian Memmot comes on."

Chaz turned off the TV. "Okay. One more question. Do you have a website?"

"The program does. Barry manages it and Stewart deals with the emails. Some listeners send a fax. The number is on the website."

"That answers that."

He reached into the drawer and handed her a new cell phone. "I've programmed it so you reach me on one, your mother on two, your sister on three and Barry Winslow on four. For now, no others can contact you on this phone.

"Keep your other phone and answer it only if you can identify the caller. Your stalker will keep phoning you on it and your landline, leaving messages to harass you. We'll listen to them together. In time, when you don't seem to be intimidated by these calls, this person will come out of the woodwork in more creative ways to terrify you, but we'll be ready for them."

She rubbed her temples. "I don't know how to thank you for all this."

"It's my job. Before I forget, I downloaded a ringtone on your new phone from *2001: A Space Odyssey.*"

"You did?" Her eyes lighted in genuine amusement, charming him.

He picked up his own phone and called her new number. When it rang, she laughed quietly. Chaz liked her laugh. "I thought it only appropriate. Change it if you want to. It won't hurt my feelings," he teased.

"I wouldn't dream of it."

Once again he was enjoying this time with her too much and needed to concentrate on the next order of business. "Is there a paranormal conference coming up soon you were planning to attend?"

"Next Friday in Albuquerque. In runs the whole weekend. But now that this has happened, I—"

"You're going to go," he informed her without preamble. "I'll be attending it with you because I believe your stalker will be there. We can do this two ways. I can show up as a friend of yours who's interested in the paranormal, or I will come with you as your new fiancé. I'd prefer the latter."

Chaz watched her eyes turn a darker shade of blue, no doubt from shock. *"Fiancé?"*

"I need to get into your world as fast as possible, Lacey. It's my opinion this stalker has harbored a deep-seated jealousy of you, either personally, because of your happy marriage and child, or professionally. Maybe both. By being your fiancé rather than just a friend with a similar interest, I would have the right to keep a closer eye on you as well as a legitimate, immediate entry into your home and life.

"If your stalker is a woman, she'll be infuriated that you've found a new love interest. If your stalker is a man, he'll hate the fact that you have a fiancé and are in love again. In either case the engagement will frustrate his or her plans."

Her hand tightened around her purse. "I suppose you're right. But if the stalker has been watching me every minute, won't he or she know our engagement's a lie?"

"Yes, and it will anger him enough that he'll make a costly mistake. But if this person hasn't been able to spy on you all the time, then he'll have to believe it. I'm planning on the unexpected engagement to infuriate him and he'll eventually show his hand. That's what I'll be waiting for. Either way, we can't lose."

She stared at him as if she'd never seen him before. "How would we explain how we got together?"

At least Lacey hadn't said no yet. He was convinced an engagement would bring things to a head sooner. When Roman Lufka had taken on a stalking case years ago, he'd gone undercover as Brittany's husband. The action had resulted in a quick capture of the culprit. It had also resulted in a real marriage taking place.

Chaz had decided to take a leaf out of his boss's book. Not quite as drastic as pretending to be Lacey's husband, but it would have the same effect on the stalker.

"That part's easy. You'll introduce me as Chaz Roylance, a guy who grew up in Long Beach and played football with your husband in high school. We were good friends, but lost track when he went into the Coast Guard. I saw the obituary in the paper and met you at the viewing. Before you moved back to Salt Lake, I came to see you several times. After that I flew up for visits.

"We've spent a lot of private time together so I could get to know you and Abby better. One thing has led to another, but we haven't told people how we feel. I finally quit my landscaping business in Long Beach and moved here. While I've been staying with you, we've gotten engaged, but we haven't made definite wedding plans yet because your daughter has to get used to the idea first."

Her head flew back, causing that wave of red-gold hair to settle on her shoulders. "So…you're planning to stay at my condo?" Maybe it wasn't panic, but he saw some emotion resembling it in her expression.

"Starting tonight," he informed her. "We'll let people know I'm looking for a home to buy for us while I get my landscaping business started here. I don't think any of your friends will recognize me, since I've only lived here a year and I've kept a low profile." He could read her mind though she wasn't saying anything. "I've already cased your place from the outside and will throw down an air mattress and sleeping bag on your back deck."

She bit her lip. "I wouldn't let you stay out there."

"Most of my time in the SEALs I slept outside and liked it. You and your family will be able to carry on with your life and hardly know I'm there. But if you'd prefer not to go with an engagement, then tell me now and I'll work out a different plan for us. The decision is up to you."

He heard her suck in her breath. "I have to admit it would be a huge relief to know you're on the premises at night."

"I'll feel better about it, too. Is that a yes?" he prodded.

"Yes," she whispered after a sustained silence.

"Do you have those family photos for me?"

"Oh, yes. I wrote names and relationships on the backs." She pulled a manila envelope out of her bag.

"I'll scan them so they can be emailed to the crew.

Be assured I'll return them tomorrow. What I'm going to do now is run you back to the supermarket. After you're home, I want you to make out that list of people I was talking about. Put down everyone you can think of, along with the core group. Tell me as much about them as you can, including phone numbers, email and home addresses. If you have pictures, attach them."

"I have a picture of the core group from the convention two months ago."

"That's even better." He got to his feet. "What time will you put your daughter to bed this evening?"

"Seven, but it usually takes twenty minutes to settle her."

"In that case I'll be there at seven-thirty with Chinese takeout, unless you prefer something else."

She looked surprised. "No. I love it."

Good. "While we eat, we'll put in a session. Tomorrow morning you can introduce me to Abby. The faster we work together, the faster we'll catch this perpetrator. Go ahead and let your mother know you'll be picking up that salad in a few minutes."

As LACEY GLANCED AT CHAZ, who'd driven her to the rear of the supermarket's loading dock, she saw that a sober expression had entered his eyes, muting the vibrant green-and-yellow color to a nondescript hazel.

"See you tonight." His deep voice resonated inside her. "Before I forget, I have something for you." He reached into his back pocket and pulled out a beautiful one-carat diamond with a smaller diamond on either side set in yellow gold. "This isn't real, but you wouldn't know it without a jeweler's loupe."

In a daze, Lacey took the ring from him. The reality

of it sent her thoughts back to the night Ted had slipped the ring he'd bought for her on her finger, promising to love her till the day he died. Her darling husband... He'd died way too soon.

Now here she was with a fake engagement ring handed to her by this remarkable P.I. while he tried to find out who was stalking her. She felt as if she was living some strange dream.

"Once we catch your stalker—which I suspect will happen before long—you can tell everyone the truth and they'll all understand the reason for the deception. Let your mother know that while we're in New Mexico, she'll have twenty-four-hour surveillance outside her house."

"Thank you," she whispered. Grasping the ring in her palm, Lacey jumped out of the car, feeling his gaze on her back as she pushed open the metal door. Once inside the store, she stared at the ring burning its shape into her skin.

She couldn't believe she'd agreed to this arrangement with a virtual stranger, but Chaz was the expert and everything he'd said had made a certain kind of sense. In truth she wouldn't dare consider going to Albuquerque if he weren't going to be right there at her side. He believed her stalker would be there and thought this was the best way to handle the situation. If she didn't have faith in him, then what else was there?

He's putting his own life in danger to protect you, and believes this is the best way, Lacey.

Without any more hesitation, she put the ring on her left ring finger. It fit! Naturally it did. Chaz Roylance knew exactly what he was doing at all times. She'd never met anyone who possessed such innate confidence. He made her feel safe in a way no one else ever had before. Almost as if she was cherished and—

"Can I help you with something?" an employee spoke up, breaking in on her train of thought.

"Oh…yes…I came back here for a fruit salad."

"We've put some on the cart over there. Take your pick."

"Thank you."

Lacey chose one and headed for the checkout counter at the front of the store, but she felt weak in the legs.

For the first time since the phone threat on her landline, the sensation had little to do with fear of her stalker. Her new, temporary fiancé possessed a masculine appeal strong enough to have thrown her senses into chaos from the first moment. As she walked out to her car, she had to admit that the chemistry missing when she'd been around other men was so thick in his presence she was drowning in it.

"You're back, Mommy!"

"Of course I'm back, honey."

"How did it go?" her mom asked after Lacey had slipped in next to Abby and kissed her.

"*This* is how it went." She sat forward and put her left hand over her mother's shoulder so she could see the ring. "Chaz is pretending to be my fiancé from California who's staying with me and Abby. He says he'll sleep out on the back deck. It's for our protection, and also to enrage the stalker. Chaz believes he'll trap him sooner this way."

"That makes a lot of sense."

"The diamonds aren't real."

"They look authentic to me, which is the only thing that matters. In my opinion it's a brilliant plan, honey.

Now you won't be alone while this menace lays his trap. Nothing could make me happier," her mother said before driving them to Lacey's condo.

"Chaz is going to attend the Albuquerque paranormal conference with me so he can meet everyone."

"In that case I'll tend Abby. Before all this happened, I was already planning to."

"I know. Thank you so much, Mom. I don't know what I'd do without you. Chaz will assign someone to guard you and Abby and Ruth while we're gone." She had to take another quick breath. "If you talk to Ruth before I do, tell her we'll be having a visitor at night at the condo for a while. He wants us to go about our business as if he weren't there."

"Though she'll pretend otherwise, you know this is a frightening experience for Ruth."

"I know. I also realize this is frightening for you, too, Mom. I'm so sorry."

"Honey, this isn't your fault."

"If I didn't have a radio show, it wouldn't have happened."

"You don't know that. Chaz told me these kinds of cases happen for all sorts of reasons. Do you believe he can catch this person?"

"Yes. He's...incredible."

"I agree, so let's stop talking about being sorry."

"Okay."

Lacey got out of the Buick and unfastened Abby from the car seat. After waving her mother off, she hurried toward the stairs, juggling her daughter and the sack containing the salad. She still couldn't comprehend how much her life had changed since that first phone threat the other morning.

Luckily Abby's needs didn't leave her much time to ponder what was happening. They played games, then came her dinner and bath. Her daughter noticed the engagement ring and tried it on several times. Anything that sparkled caught her eye. Lacey explained that a friend named Chaz had given it to her. Once Abby was in her jammies, they went through her bedtime ritual until she fell asleep.

Lacey tiptoed out of the bedroom and hurried into the bathroom to freshen her lipstick and brush her hair. Chaz would be here any second. It surprised her how she was counting the minutes. She'd set up her laptop on the dining room table. Her family room was a combination eating area and kitchen along with an entertainment center and TV. Lacey liked the open arrangement.

Waiting for Chaz to arrive, she continued to compile a list of names, but it was by no means complete. When her cell phone rang with its new music, she jumped and pulled it out of her pocket. It was Chaz. Her pulse sped up. "Hello?"

"Hi. I'm outside the door, but didn't want to ring the bell and chance waking up your daughter."

Lacey appreciated his thoughtfulness. "I'll be right there." She clicked off and rushed to the small foyer to open the door. Warm air, still in the low eighties, filled the condo with its scent of honeysuckle. It was that *summer* smell she loved so much.

Chaz handed her their sack of food before he stepped inside wearing a backpack. He'd brought a bedroll and an inflatable air mattress. After locking the door behind him, she told him to put everything on the living room couch.

He'd showered and changed clothes. Tonight he had on a silky dark chocolate-colored shirt and tan chinos. She averted her eyes to keep from staring. "Come into the family room. I thought that would be the best place to work. Are you hungry?"

"Starving." He followed her into the other room where she put the sack of Chinese takeout on the table.

"So am I. I'll dish everything up right now."

He darted her a glance. "While you do that, I'll take a look around," he said quietly. "If by any chance your stalker broke into your condo to plant cameras or listening devices, I'll find them."

Lacey remembered her mother telling her to whisper because their voices might be picked up.

"Go ahead. Abby's a sound sleeper, but even if you disturb her, I don't mind. The thought of being spied on is terrifying."

"I'll be careful not to waken her."

By the time he'd come back to the family room and inspected it as well, she had everything ready, including the fruit salad and coffee.

"The place is clean in more ways than one."

"That's a huge relief…in more ways than one," she added. He chuckled and sat down opposite her. "Thank you for the food, Chaz. It's smells delicious."

"My pleasure. Your little girl looks like an angel sleeping in there." His gaze roved over her hair before he started eating. "It's not hard to tell you're her mommy."

"Nope. We stand out." She bit into an egg roll. "My daughter will have to learn to live with the curly red hair the way I did. Ted wanted to name her Anne, with an *e*."

"Of Green Gables, I presume."

They both laughed.

"You have a lovely condo. I like the Swedish-modern motif."

"Thanks. I plan to buy a real home in a few years, but this suits my needs right now."

"I know what you mean. I'm in a condo, too."

"Did you move here recently?"

"About a year ago."

"Where are you from?" Now that they were pretending to be engaged, she realized she needed some background on him. The truth was, she had a great curiosity about him. It came as a shock considering she'd thought Ted's death had permanently taken away her interest in other men. But there was something about Chaz....

"I was born and raised in Tucson, Arizona. After my wife died, I became a navy SEAL. After close to a decade I got out and joined Roman's P.I. firm. Only a few people know I was a SEAL. That's for your ears only. Not because it's a secret, but because I'm a private person and prefer not to talk about it."

So was she. "Understood." It explained so much about him. She opened a fortune cookie. Good luck was coming her way. With Chaz helping her, she could believe it was true. "Are SEALs allowed to have longer hair?" He was so attractive, the question just popped out, causing her to blush.

He smiled at her over the rim of his coffee cup. "No. After I left the service I let it grow again."

The SEALs had an extraordinary reputation for being the most highly skilled and trained amphibious units in the world. She'd talked to several who'd called in to her show before and knew they were deployed for hostage rescues and counterterrorism.

Until now, Lacey had assumed Chaz had come from a background in law enforcement. It made her shiver just to imagine the situations he would have been in as a SEAL.

"Why did you come to Salt Lake?"

"Before my wife passed away, I brought her to the Huntsman Cancer Institute, hoping for a cure. It didn't happen, but Salt Lake has mountains and deserts and four distinct seasons, which I like, so I gravitated back here. However, I'm finding that condo living is getting old. No place to put all the things I have in storage. No yard."

"Tell me about it. I've got boxes and boxes of books and DVDs of old sci-fi TV shows stored, too." As they talked, she realized that if she didn't keep her wits about her, she might forget why he was here.

"Forgive me for causing you any undue stress, but do you have a guest book signed by people who came to your husband's viewing and funeral?"

The mention brought back painful memories, but she had to admit they hadn't been surfacing quite as often these days as they had in the first few months after Ted's death. She realized Chaz needed everything she could provide to do a thorough investigation on her case. "Yes. I'll get it."

"Is it in storage?" he asked quietly.

She bit her lip. "No. Everything's still on a shelf in my closet with a few of the programs from the funeral."

"I'd like to look at one of those, too."

"Of course. I'll get everything for you before I go to bed. By the way, please feel free to use the guest bedroom. I'll show you. Ruth doesn't stay here on weekends. The rest of the time you can sleep on the Hide-A-Bed couch in the family room."

He smiled. "That's very considerate of you. Tell you what, if there's a summer storm that threatens to drench me, I'll take you up on your offer. Otherwise, I like sleeping outside. I can hear things better."

Like her stalker creeping around...

After they finished eating, she got up to clear the table. He helped her, but she wished he wouldn't because he stood too close to her at the sink and she was afraid he could hear her heart thudding like a jackhammer. In a few minutes she sat down again and pulled the laptop toward her.

"I've been making up that list of people you asked for."

He poured himself another cup of coffee. "Let me hear what you have on your core group."

She handed him the big photograph. "I listed their names in order from right to left."

He studied it as she read him the information. After listening, he said, "You travel in some impressive circles. I've heard of several of these people. It appears they all have substantial credentials and in some cases have put in years at their various professions."

"They're exceptional. That's why it's so hard to imagine any of them having a dark side."

Chaz put the photo down. "Unfortunately all human beings have that potential. Go ahead and tell me about the rest of the people on your list."

Lacey read the sketches. None of them sounded or seemed capable of doing harm to anyone, let alone to her. She couldn't fathom it, but the fact remained some-one was out to kill her.

"So far you've talked about colleagues and college personnel, the people at your former radio station, friends you and your husband did things with socially, church friends, extended family on both sides. You've made a good beginning. Now I need the names of your neighbors here in the complex, your landlord."

"Of course. I forgot all about that."

"Don't worry. It's my job to help you remember. What about childhood friends?"

She blinked. "You mean like an old girlfriend?"

Chaz nodded. "And guy friends. Some you might have played Kick the Can with." He lounged against the counter drinking the hot liquid.

"No guy friends like that. Just Jenny and Brenda, who were my two closest friends from grade school, and still are my very best friends. I forgot to put their names down. They come to as many paranormal con-ferences as they can. The three of us were science-fiction nuts from the beginning. We formed a club in high school our sophomore year called the Bengal Al-golans."

A heart-stopping smile started at one corner of his mouth. "How many belonged to *your* club?"

She laughed because he knew too much about her already. "Eight on a good month. We'd read science-fiction stories out loud and watch science-fiction mov-ies. After I got my driver's license, we would head out to Great Salt Lake with my telescope."

His dark brows lifted. "A good one?"

"Very good. Expensive. My parents gave it to me on

my fourteenth birthday because they knew how much I loved astronomy."

"I read your dedication to them in your book. Your sentiments were understandable."

Lacey nodded. "Daddy died of a lung clot soon after that." Her eyelids prickled. "Anyway, when the club went to the lake, we'd roast hot dogs and look for meteors coming close to Earth."

"For Percy?" he prodded.

Lacey loved that he knew so much about her novel, but she realized he'd read it as part of his investigation, no other reason.

"The birth of my restless Algolan happened the first night we were out there and I saw a shooting star spike through the heavens like a javelin. As I watched, I thought, what if that star was really a meteor that someone from outer space was riding to reach Earth?

"At first I wrote Percy landing in Great Salt Lake, but I soon discovered the lake was too small to give him enough scope for all his underwater powers. Worse, the heavy salt water clogged up the holes behind his ears, interfering with his transmissions to and from Algol."

Something flickered in the recesses of Chaz's eyes. "Your mind continues to fascinate me. So do your teenage exploits. While some teens are out at night getting into earthly trouble, you and your friends were out daring aliens to come and visit. Put your friends' names on the list with phones and addresses."

"Except for Jenny and Brenda, I haven't seen those other kids from the club since we all graduated from high school."

"I still want a full list," he insisted.

Her throat tightened. "But surely you don't think

any of them would—" She stopped midsentence. Now that she knew he'd been a SEAL for the past ten years, she realized he would be thorough to the extreme, considering every possibility in order to save her life. She should be thankful for that. She *was* thankful.

Taking a quick second breath, she typed in all the names and added the information he'd asked for. "I'll print the list for you now."

"While you do that, I'll leave to get another key made for your front door. When I come back later on tonight, I'll be able to slip into the condo without disturbing you."

"Oh—" She'd forgotten about giving him a key. Of course he'd need one.

Her purse was on the counter. She jumped up from the table and walked over to get it. After finding the keys, she took the one in question off the ring. "I'm sure you're anxious to get going." Lacey didn't want him to think she was hoping he'd stay longer, but when she handed the key to him, he looked at her so strangely. "What is it, Chaz? Have you thought of something else?"

"No. This will do for now," he said, but he sounded far away. When they reached the front door, he turned to her. "What's your schedule like tomorrow?"

"I was planning to take Abby to Mother's and stay for lunch."

He nodded. "I'll be out of your condo early in the morning, so if you're not up when I come back tonight, we'll touch base tomorrow and get together." After a slight pause he added, "I need to get acquainted with Abby and we have more to discuss. For your information, I listened to the message on your landline in the bedroom earlier."

"I didn't realize." The mention of it made her feel ill.

"I traced the call. It came from a public phone at a casino in Reno, Nevada. Think about anyone you know who might have visited there recently. Your stalker gets around. Good night."

"Good night."

Lacey locked the door behind him before sagging against it. She couldn't think who would have been in·Reno or anywhere near there. The deeper timbre of his voice had sent a little shiver down her spine. In a minute she pulled herself together and retrieved her laptop.

Being as quiet as possible, she hurried through the condo to her bedroom. While she printed the file she'd been creating, she went to her closet for the funeral guest book and program he'd requested.

Her high school and college yearbooks were on the same shelf, along with some of her old elementary school yearbooks and scrapbooks. She decided to get everything down for him. She'd put all the items on the dining room table for him to study.

There was no point in waiting up for him. It was none of her business where he was headed after he made the key, or for how long he'd be gone. He could come and go without worry since he had a crew who kept her and the condo under constant surveillance, but she'd sensed he was eager to get going.

He probably had a date. It was the weekend, after all. *And he was gorgeous.* Few women would be immune to him.

Chapter Four

Chaz left Lacey's condo and walked out to the guest parking area, nodding to Adam who was on duty in an unmarked van in guest parking. On a purely selfish level, Chaz hadn't been ready to leave her. But the fact that she'd jumped up so fast to make him a hard copy of her list before she went to bed had prompted him to say good-night. Lacey was tired, of course. Besides being a busy mother and doing a radio show, he knew she had to be emotionally exhausted from fear.

By the time he'd driven off, he had to admit that the strong attraction he felt for her when they were in the same room had him tied in knots. What if the attraction was only on his part?

Her husband hadn't been gone that long. The questions he'd asked her, the mention of the funeral guest book had disturbed her. As she'd told him, she couldn't imagine being with another man. From a professional standpoint, her disinterest in men worked in his favor, but this was one time when he wished the reverse were true.

Since joining Roman's firm, Chaz had been with other women, but he'd never gotten personally involved with a client. It went against the rules. But this case seemed to have been different from the outset. He'd taken it on for reasons tied to that black period in the SEALs, and now he was pretending to be her fiancé.

After spending time with Lacey Pomeroy, more than ever he wanted to catch the person tormenting her. It was fast becoming his raison d'être. But he needed to be careful that *she* wasn't becoming someone of importance to him on a personal level. If he let that happen, then he could lose his edge. Physical attraction was one thing. Emotional involvement was another. Neither had any place in his life while he was trying to catch her stalker.

But after Chaz had gone back to the office and had let himself into the shop to make another front-door key on their machine, he liked the idea that he would be returning to her condo for the night. The thought of his own sterile living quarters left him numb.

An hour later, all was quiet when Chaz used the new key to enter Lacey's place. Even if she wasn't asleep, she'd gone to bed.

He went out onto the deck to inflate his mattress, then threw his sleeping bag and pillow on top of it. Knowing he wasn't tired enough to sleep yet, he went back to the family room where she'd put the printouts and funeral guest book on the table. It pleased him to see the pile of yearbooks and photo albums with them.

On top of the big ones—including a few of her husband's, who'd apparently attended the University of Southern California—there were some brochurelike yearbooks with Lacey's name written on the covers. These would contain valuable information.

Though he could feel his work calling to him, Chaz found himself reaching for the reader he'd left on the table. He couldn't kid himself about certain feelings Lacey had aroused in him on several levels. Those feelings had grabbed hold and weren't about to go away. With a sense of excitement, he scrolled to chapter two of the Stargrazer book, eager to read more.

He soon discovered this was where the female earthling named Olivia came into the story. She was on her way to boarding school in Europe and was in her cabin aboard ship, typing an email on her laptop because she'd just undergone a bizarre incident.

Brenda—at first I thought it was a trick of light, but now I'm positive I saw an angel out on deck!

Chaz rubbed his bottom lip with his thumb. Brenda was the name of one of Lacey's oldest friends. It had crept into her book. What could be more natural? Much as he wanted to go on reading, he was curious to know more about her friend.

He turned off the reader and reached for the list of names and information she'd given him.

Brenda Halverson Nichols. Twenty-eight. Sandy, Utah, address. Parents' home in Cottonwood Heights. Graduate of Bengal High School. Married to attorney Robert. Graduated from University of Utah with master's in theater arts. Part-time actress in various theaters around Salt Lake Valley. Sci-fi lover.

Sandy and Cottonwood Heights were next door to each other in terms of neighborhoods. Chaz's gaze lit on her other friend's name.

Jennifer Bradford West. Twenty-eight. Los Angeles, California, address. Parents' home in Cottonwood Heights. Graduate of Bengal High School. Divorced.

Ph.D. from the University of Southern California, Los Angeles. Professor of English literature at UCLA. Sci-fi lover.

As he'd asked, Lacey had also written down the names of the other six students who'd belonged to the Bengal Algolans Club.

Curious to put names with faces, he opened one of the elementary school yearbooks first. It contained a series of schoolroom pictures taken with the individual teachers. Chaz found Lacey Garvey's name in the third-grade photograph.

She sat in the front row, a cute little redhead with curly locks, reminding him of her daughter. In the second row he spotted Jennifer Bradford. Her blond hair had been put in French braids. At the other end of the row sat a taller brunette with short pixielike hair named Brenda Halverson.

Going from that yearbook, he searched for Lacey's Bengal High School yearbook when she would have been a sophomore. After turning to the section listing the school clubs, he found a half page devoted to the Bengal Algolans Club showing Lacey Garvey as president, looking through her telescope. It resembled the picture of her at the back of her published novel where she had long hair.

Also in the picture were Jennifer, Brenda and six other students, four females and two males. He checked the names against the list she'd given him. Everything lined up exactly as she'd presented it.

The index at the back of the yearbook listed all the names and the pages where the students' pictures could be found. He found four more listings for Lacey: one as a member of the sophomore class, one as a member of the literary club, another in the science club and the last as a reporter for the school newspaper. She'd been a busy girl and obviously an outstanding one.

Brenda had more pictures besides being in the Algolan club. She was an officer in the drama club, a member of the debate club and she belonged to the literary club.

His search for Jennifer turned up three listings of photos besides the yearbook picture. She'd been an officer in the literary club, a member of the Algolan club and sang in the girls' choir.

He put that yearbook aside and reached for Lacey's senior yearbook. The index listed seven pages by her name. Besides being an officer in her favorite clubs, she'd been the top physics student in the state of Utah and had received the Sterling Scholar award. A four-point student, she'd also been the senior-class valedictorian. Last but not least, she'd received a full academic scholarship to Stanford University.

Chaz stared into space. Someone out there in the cosmos hated the fact that Lacey Pomeroy was the girl who had everything.

Maybe it was a man deeply twisted by insecurity who knew she would never give him a moment's notice. Maybe it was a scarred woman begging for the attention Lacey constantly received without even thinking about it.

Out of curiosity he looked up her sister's picture. She would have been a sophomore when Lacey was a senior. All the Garvey women were attractive. Ruth looked the most like their mother. She had been in the ski club and the hiking club.

Lacey resembled her redheaded father. Chaz noticed from the family photographs that Mr. Garvey's deceased brother had been redheaded, too.

He shut that yearbook before turning to the guest book from her husband's funeral. After cross-checking the names against the ones on her list of friends and associates, he made a startling discovery. It appeared that at least ninety percent of the people on her list had either attended the viewing or the funeral itself.

Considering the distances most of them had to travel to Long Beach, the loyalty and devotion to her and her husband was phenomenal. Except of course for the one person who put that death threat on her windshield and might—or might not—have signed the guest book.

He made more notes to himself. Finally he put everything to do with the case in his backpack and carried it out to the deck where he could smell honeysuckle. The scent took him to an earlier period in his life when he had few worries and hormones filled him with longings. This was one of those incredible summer nights.

No one was about outside. Ten minutes later his mind was still percolating with ideas. On a personal level, it was a good thing he didn't have to wait any longer than the rest of the night to see Lacey again. Professionally, he had a dozen new questions to ask her.

When morning came he left the condo early, waving to Tom, who'd taken over for Adam. Chaz drove to his own place to shower and eat breakfast. At 9:00 a.m. he phoned Lacey. Upon answering, she sounded slightly breathless. "Chaz?"

"Good morning."

"You sound wide awake. When did you leave the condo?"

"At six-thirty. I left your door key on the kitchen counter."

"I saw it. Thank you."

"I would have put all your yearbooks away, but didn't know where you keep them."

"No problem. I've already reshelved them in the closet."

"They were a great help. I know you're going over to your mother's with Abby, but I need a question answered. Do you have a minute or are you too busy with her to talk?"

"I can do both. She's playing with her buckets."

"How does one do that?"

"They're different sizes. You fit them into each other. She's still having problems with the medium-size ones, a little matter of visual perception." So spoke the physicist. "But it keeps her busy for five minutes at a time."

He chuckled. "Tell me something. Why did you pick Brenda to be in your book? I've just gotten to the part where Olivia tells her friend she's seen an angel. At the time you were writing your novel, why didn't you choose a name from among your other friends? For instance the other girls in the Algolan club?"

"The Brenda in my novel wasn't named for my friend. That was just a coincidence. It was named for my favorite female Hollywood actress at the time, Brenda Joyce. That wasn't her real name, but the point is, she played opposite Johnny Weissmuller and Lex Barker in the first Tarzan movies.

"I loved Edgar Rice Burroughs's books and watched the films. A lot of people don't know that before he created Tarzan, he wrote all kinds of science fiction with a romantic element I devoured. There was one series called Under the Moons of Mars. It's about a guy named John Carter who lies dying in a cave in Arizona—your home state, as I recall—and he finds his spirit staring down at his body.

"He looks up at the planet Mars and he suddenly finds himself on the Red Planet where he's thrust in the middle of different tribes fighting each other while the air on their planet is running out. Those Barsoom books were the best series! I would always picture Brenda Joyce as one of the Red Planet maidens. She had beautiful blond hair. I hated my hair and dreamed about looking just like her."

Chaz had news for her. Lacey had enough beauty with her face and flame-colored tresses to fill a thousand men's dreams. The excitement in her voice infected him. "Does Brenda know the story behind your choice of the name Brenda?"

"I don't know if we ever talked about it. She and Jen read a lot of the stuff I read and they both knew how much I loved Brenda Joyce."

He sipped his coffee. "Thanks for putting out those yearbooks. They helped me fit names and faces together. I noticed from your sophomore yearbook that you and your friends belonged to the literary club. What went on there exactly?"

"A group of about twenty sophomores, juniors and seniors got together twice a month after school to write short stories and poetry. The head of the English department coached us and then chose the best writings to feature in a magazine put out for the student body at the end of the year."

"How many of your stories made it?"

"Two of them."

"Science fiction, of course."

"Of course." Her laughter brought a smile to his face. "One was about a family that lived in a black hole."

Unbelievable. "And the other?"

"It was a story about Galileo. While he was looking through the lens on the long telescope he built, he suddenly found himself trillions of light-years away. He had all sorts of adventures, but when he returned to Earth, no one believed him."

"I want to read both stories."

"They're in one of those famous boxes in storage."

"We'll have to dig them out. What about your friends' stories?"

"Jenny had several accepted. Brenda wrote a series of poems, but the teacher didn't put them in, which was a shame."

After swallowing the last of his brew he said, "Did you ever read parts of the Stargrazer to the students in the literary club while you were writing your novel?"

"Heavens, no!"

Her reaction surprised him. "Not even to your two best friends?"

"Never. I was too scared."

"Scared?"

"Yes! I was afraid they'd laugh. That novel was a secret. One day I asked the school librarian if there was a book that listed a lot of publishers. She found me one called *Writers' Market*. In there I discovered various publishing houses dealing with all genres of fiction and nonfiction.

"I studied it for days and days and finally sent my story to some different editors of young-adult fantasy fiction who didn't require an agent. When I got a letter back from one of them telling me they were interested, I showed the letter to my mom."

"That's the first she'd heard?" Chaz was incredulous.

"Well, my parents knew I loved to write, but I didn't tell them about that particular story. By then Dad had passed away."

"He would have been very proud of you."

"Thanks. I loved him so much."

"When your book came out, did you give your girl-friends a copy?"

"No. By that time I'd left for Stanford. How would it have looked if I'd said, 'Hey, everyone, see what I wrote while I was in high school!'"

"But what about other people?"

"Not everyone likes science fiction. Did you?"

"Maybe not then."

She chuckled. "It's okay that you didn't like it, then or now."

"I'm crazy about the Stargrazer," he declared and meant it.

"I'm glad, but the truth is, I would never force my writing on anyone."

Lacey didn't have an ego. "So Jenny and Brenda probably went out to buy a copy. What did they say when they read it?"

"By that time Jenny was at UCLA."

"Was she given a scholarship like you?"

"No. She phoned to congratulate me and told me she was blabbing it up to everyone in the English depart-ment down there. She was very sweet. As for Brenda, when I was in Salt Lake for Christmas break, she came over to my mom's house with a box of books and asked me to autograph them so she could give them out to her family and friends. She said she was madly in love with Percy."

"She and Roseanne," he teased. "I'm sure that was all very gratifying to hear."

"Coming from my closest friends, you can't imagine."

"When Brenda read your book for the first time, do you think she might have thought you named Brenda after her, rather than the actress?"

"Maybe. I simply don't know."

Chaz pondered her comment. Whatever Brenda thought, she hadn't been the one to write a novel that got published. And if she knew Lacey had put in the name Brenda in honor of Brenda Joyce, she might have taken it as a slight.

Acid on the wound because Brenda hadn't been published in the school magazine? Another failure in her eyes because she hadn't written the bestselling novel created by her best friend? One who'd kept it a secret until it came out and became a sensation?

His thoughts switched to Jennifer. Her name hadn't been mentioned in the book. Did it bother her that Brenda's name had slipped in? Jenny was an English professor. If she'd always wanted to teach English at the college level, then it meant she had to publish to build tenure.

It might have been a blow to learn that Lacey had gotten published while she was still in high school and had never told anyone. A big enough blow for seeds of envy to burst out of control?

While his mind kept coming up with more thoughts

and questions, she said, "Do you mind if I ask why you want to know?"

"It's not a case of minding, Lacey. Right now my thoughts are darting to and fro about the people on your list and I'm thinking out loud. When was the last time you saw Jenny?"

"At a paranormal conference in Houston in April. Mother watched Abby."

"What about Brenda?"

"She went, too. We flew down together."

"Does she have children?"

"Not yet, but they're trying."

Chaz paced the floor. "Have you seen Jenny since then?"

"No. We've had too many deadlines and she lives in Los Angeles."

"How about Brenda? How often do you see her?"

"Every two weeks or so. Sometimes not that often if she's doing a play. She came over last Saturday and we watched some DVDs of *Otherworld*. I'd ordered them off the internet."

"I haven't heard of that show."

"It was a sci-fi series made for TV years ago, but only played for one season. We loved it."

"You'll have to put it on for me to watch."

"Anytime."

"I'm going to take you up on that. Now go enjoy your daughter and call me later after you're home from your mother's. Then I'll come over."

"We'll be back by four. Mom has plans with her church group for the rest of the evening."

"In that case I'll be there then. I'm anxious to meet Abby and get to know her while we talk about the case."

"I'll be here and supply the leftovers from dinner. Mother's lamb roast is to die for."

"You shouldn't have told me," he murmured. "I'll be salivating all day."

He hung up, wondering how he was going to make it until he could be with her later. At the same time he was trying to wrap his mind around the idea of professional envy being a motive for the death threats. It was a thought he'd entertained from the first moment he'd heard Lacey had her own radio show.

Brenda Halverson Nichols lived right here in Salt Lake. She and Lacey had been joined at the hip from childhood. She'd signed the guest book at the funeral. Brenda was supposed to be one of Lacey's best friends, yet Lacey hadn't said anything to her or Jenny about her novel until after she'd gotten published. Not only published, but honored with prestigious awards that led to a sci-fi radio show.

Were either of her friends the type who believed a real friend shared *everything?* What was the old adage about jealousy? It's a tiger that tears not only its prey, but also its own raging heart.

If Brenda were an actress at the very top of her game, why wasn't she onstage in New York instead of having to settle for less by doing part-time theater here in Salt Lake? Over the past six years of attending various sci-fi conventions with Lacey, who'd become so prominent, had Brenda developed a raging heart from coming in second best on all fronts?

Was there enough anger to welcome Ted's death and

go gleefully after Lacey, whose life no longer looked so rosy without her husband? How would she react when she heard Lacey was engaged? For the moment, Brenda Nichols was emerging at the top of his list of possible suspects.

Jennifer came a close second. She'd been at the funeral. Though she'd distinguished herself, she didn't have Lacey's celebrity status. A professor at UCLA was impressive, yet she wasn't the girl who'd won a four-year academic scholarship to Stanford. Her marriage had ended in divorce.

Three friends from childhood, yet only one shining star nationally acclaimed in radio and fiction writing. Interesting that of the three of them, Lacey was the only one with a child. A sweet little daughter any would-be mother would yearn to call her own.

But these were early days and he knew this was only the tip of the iceberg.

After reaching his office, questions continued to bombard Chaz while he dug up more information on her core group of friends he'd be meeting next weekend. The knowledge that he'd be spending the weekend with her brightened his mood despite the seriousness of the case.

Chapter Five

Despite the ever-present menace, Lacey returned to her condo at ten to four, more excited than she should have been because Chaz would be arriving shortly. She moved Abby's small white table and chair from her bedroom into the family room, where she could draw on her pad with her colored markers. That way she could see her mommy working at the dining room table.

Her little girl loved to dance and wear frilly skirts. As soon as they walked in the door, Abby ran to her room to play dress-up. She added her butterfly wings and a garland, which she plopped at a tilted angle on top of her curly red hair. When she smiled at Lacey with Ted's light blue eyes, she melted Lacey's heart.

Earlier Lacey's mother had helped paint Abby's finger- and toenails a scarlet pink. Abby had covered both arms with red ink valentine tattoos from her little set of stamps. Her play lipstick went beyond the lines of her rosebud mouth. That was the sight to greet Chaz when Lacey let him in the condo. He carried his backpack and wore jeans and a blue T-shirt revealing a well-defined chest.

Her daughter got up, carrying her magic wand, and walked over to them. Lacey looked down at her.

"Honey? This is my friend Chaz. He was the one who gave me this ring. Can you say hello to him?"

"Hello," she said in a small voice.

While Lacey shut and locked the front door, Chaz got down on his haunches. The smile in his eyes matched the one on his striking features. "Hi. What's your name, sweetheart?"

"Abby."

"Are you a princess?"

"Yes. I'm Princess Butterfly Abby. I can fly." With that, she ran around in her bare feet, flinging her arms.

Chaz's deep-throated laughter filled the condo. Lacey loved his laugh. Abby loved the attention. She circled the room several times, then stopped in front of him. "Abracadabra," she said, pointing her wand at him. "You're a frog!"

"Don't feel slighted," Lacey whispered to him. In a louder voice she said, "Abby? Go get Mr. Frog and show Chaz."

"Okay. Don't leave, Mommy."

"I won't."

Still staying in character, she flew down the hall. Chaz's gaze swerved to Lacey's. His eyes were dancing. "I've never seen such a cute little girl in my life."

Lacey almost said she'd never seen such a gorgeous man in her life, but Abby saved her from making a complete fool of herself by running back into the living room. She stood in front of Chaz, hugging her frog tightly.

"He's your favorite animal, isn't he, honey?" Lacey said.

Abby nodded.

"What does Mr. Frog say?" he asked her.

She made the best frog sounds she could with all the intensity she possessed. Lacey had been working on it with her. Again Chaz laughed and clapped his hands as if she'd given a marvelous performance. "You sound just like a frog. Come on over to the couch. I have a present for you."

That word caught her attention in a hurry. "What is it?" She followed him.

He sat down and pulled a doll out of his backpack. The minute Lacey saw it, she let out a little cry of delight. "A nesting doll—"

Chaz flicked her a glance. "My boss's wife says she raised their daughter on one of these. When you told me about the buckets, I thought Abby might like this. Roman comes from Russian descent and sent me to a shop where they're imported."

He undid the top of the doll and another doll just like it was inside. Abby stood there fascinated while he kept finding another smaller doll. When he'd finished, there were seven dolls lined up on the cushion.

"Those are going to keep you busy for a long time, honey. Can you say thank-you to Chaz?"

"Thank you, Chaz." But already she was trying to figure out how to fit all the parts together. "Look, Mommy, a teeny baby." *Teeny* was one of her favorite new words.

"Yes. Isn't she sweet? She looks just like her mommy. Come on. Let's put these on your table," Lacey suggested.

Chaz helped pick up the fourteen parts. Pretty soon Abby was working away at her new project, the frog and drawing pad forgotten. He assisted her to find the right bases for the right tops. Watching them interact caught at Lacey's heart. Abby thanked him every time he put another one together. Like Chaz, Lacey's daughter had a brand of charm that got to you.

As she stood by and watched, she sensed Abby wasn't the only one having fun. "I've warmed up your dinner, Chaz. Come into the other room whenever you're ready." As promised, she'd brought home the leftover lamb roast and everything that went with it.

The three of them spent a pleasant evening together. By the time Abby got out of the bath and put on clean jammies, she wanted Chaz to read her a story about the buzzing bee. It was one of her favorites from her birthday in May.

The week before, she'd gotten stung by a bee on her leg and needed to show Chaz and talk about it. When he turned to the last page, it made a big buzzing sound and surprised him. His exaggerated cry for Abby's benefit caused her to go into gales of laughter. She couldn't stop. He opened and closed the last page half a dozen times, delighting Lacey, too.

"Okay. It's time for bed. Say good-night to Chaz."

"G-good night, Chaz." She was still giggling.

"Good night, sweetheart. Here's Mr. Frog." He put the toy in her arms.

"Thanks." She waved bye-bye and grabbed the tiniest nesting doll before going with Lacey.

CHAZ HADN'T BEEN KIDDING when he'd told Lacey how cute her daughter was. In reality, *cute* wasn't the right description. She was adorable. Smart. Creative. Even at three years of age, she had an amazing sense of humor. With those red-gold curls bouncing just like her mother's against the pink candy-stripe pajamas, she came close to looking and acting like an enchanting angel.

When he thought of the death threats against the two of them, the blood in his veins turned to ice.

"Chaz? Is anything wrong? You have a fierce look on your face."

He jerked his head around, unaware Lacey had come back to the family room. "I want to catch the person who's threatening yours and Abby's happiness." Chaz eyed her solemnly. "She's a precious little girl."

Lacey sat down opposite him. "You made a big impression on her. Did you notice she took the baby doll to bed with her?"

He would have told her yes if her old cell phone hadn't rung. She'd left both cells on the table. "Do you recognize the caller ID?"

"No," she said, sounding frightened.

"Answer it and we'll see what happens. Be sure to put it on speakerphone."

She picked it up and clicked on. "Hello?"

"Lacey?"

"Oh, hi, Ken. I didn't realize it was you calling."

Remembering there was a Kenneth on her coregroup list, Chaz reached for the printout and read the information on him again.

"The juice went out on my cell, so I'm using the phone in the front office. I'm glad I caught you. How are you?"

"I'm good. And you?"

"Couldn't be better. Are you flying to Albuquerque this coming weekend?"

"Absolutely." Chaz watched her, noticing how hard she was trying to sound upbeat.

"That's what I wanted to hear. I was hoping you and I could go out to dinner after the seminar on Saturday night. There's this Mexican restaurant with the greatest mariachi band you ever heard."

Chaz checked his picture in the group photograph. Ken Simpson was the biochemist from Indiana and looked to be in his early forties. Was this the first time he'd asked her out?

"Ken, much as I'm flattered by the invitation, I'm afraid I can't. You see…" She lifted her eyes to Chaz. "I just got engaged."

Lacey was a remarkably quick study. Naturally she would be, with her intelligence. *And* her life on the line.

The silence coming from the other end needed no translation. Then, "You're teasing me. Right?"

"No. Why would I do that? His name is Chaz Roylance. He'll be coming with me."

"I guess I don't understand. I wanted to take you to dinner at the last conference, but when I spoke to Brenda about you, she said you needed more time because of Ted."

Lacey flinched visibly. "I didn't know you'd had a conversation with her. I'm sorry about this, Ken."

"So am I," he said with a tinge of bitterness. "I had no idea you were seeing anyone else. I guess Brenda was covering for you."

"She doesn't know about Chaz yet. You're the first person I've told besides my own family," she answered honestly.

"Is he from Salt Lake?"

"No. California."

"Someone you and Ted knew?"

The guy was starting to lose his cool. Chaz shook

his head. "Don't tell him anything else," he mouthed the words. He wanted to see just how anxious the other man would get if she refused to tell him everything.

Lacey's eyes went a smokier blue. "Ken? I have to put my daughter to bed now, but I'll look forward to seeing you at the conference."

"It's debatable whether I'll attend."

"Please don't say that. We've been friends for years. The group wouldn't be the same without you."

"Don't patronize me, Lacey. Surely you realized I was interested in you."

"As a colleague." She gripped the phone tighter. "You've always been an integral part of the group. That's why I'm hoping you'll be at the conference. I really do have to hang up now. Good night." White-faced, she rang off and jumped up from the table. She stared at Chaz in anguish.

"You handled him perfectly."

"Then it was an accident. I've never once suspected Ken wanted to take me out. I don't understand why Brenda didn't tell me."

Chaz had his own theory about that. "If there were no stalker, would you have said yes to him, if only as a friend? He's nice looking."

She shook her head so fast Chaz sensed she was telling the truth. "When he asked me to dinner just now, I was thankful to be able to tell him I was involved with someone else. I don't want a personal relationship in my life. After Ted…" Lacey stopped talking, reminding Chaz once again that deep inside she was still mourning her husband's death.

"You wrote down here that Ken's divorced. Do you know for how long?"

"I think about two years."

"Do you know the reason for it?"

"He told the group that he and his wife had irreconcilable differences. Just now he came off sounding so angry. It wasn't at all like him."

Chaz raked a hand through his hair. "Speaking from a male point of view, I would imagine he's been attracted to you for a long time and thought he finally had a chance. After what Brenda told him, finding out you're suddenly engaged would disappoint any man anxious to start a relationship with an extraordinary woman such as yourself."

She grimaced. "Extraordinarily weird, maybe. I know that's what a lot of people think about me. I never dreamed my interest in the paranormal would put me or my daughter in this kind of danger." She clutched the back of the nearest chair. "After that conversation with Ken, I guess it's possible he's been the one making those death threats."

"Possible, but not probable. I see he signed the funeral guest book. He wants to date you, not terrify you. Since this was the first time he asked you out, he didn't know you would reject him. I doubt very much he put that note under your windshield wiper, which means he didn't make the threatening calls. Remember, they're all of a piece."

Lacey's eyes flashed blue fire. "No matter the answer, you're a genius to have suggested this mock engagement. I would never have seen this side of him otherwise. What I find strange is that Brenda never told me he'd talked to her. She's had plenty of time to tell me. The last conference was in April. I'm beginning to wonder if I know anyone as well as I thought I did."

Chaz was glad to see the blinders were coming off. The more she started thinking outside the box, the more useful she would be in helping him solve her case. "You could ask her the next time you talk to her."

"I intend to."

"While we're on the subject of Brenda, I need to make a reservation to fly to New Mexico with you two."

"I'll take care of it now. You'll need a hotel room, too."

She sat back down in front of her laptop. He reached into his wallet for his credit card and handed it to her. In a few minutes she said, "It's done, but I don't think the three of us will be able to sit together."

Chaz put the card away. "I suppose I can sacrifice long enough to sit alone for the flight there. But I insist on being seated next to my fiancée for the return trip."

She blushed, bringing the color she'd lost during the conversation with Ken back to her lovely face. Her reaction secretly thrilled him because it might mean she wasn't completely disinterested.

In a lightning move she got up from the table. "Thank you for the gift for Abby," she said. The quick change in subject told him she was oddly rattled. "It went beyond your job as a P.I."

"I like doing things for little girls with bouncing curls."

Lacey averted her eyes. "You made a friend tonight."

"Your mother made a friend of me. I'll thank her later, but in the meantime please tell her how much I loved the roast. I'll eat her leftovers anytime."

She smiled. "I'll let her know. If you'll excuse me, I'm going to bed."

Chaz realized Lacey Pomeroy had a lot to think about. So did he. "I'll be heading for the deck myself in a few minutes. Get a good sleep. Remember, you're safe."

"Who keeps *you* safe?" came the question before she disappeared too fast for him to answer.

Funny, no one had ever asked him that before. It was as unexpected as she was. Unexpected, and growing on him in ways he couldn't stop even if he wanted to.

His thoughts darted to Ken, the first of her core group to be knocked sideways by the news of her recent engagement. Pleased that his plan had already produced a reaction, Chaz decided to celebrate. What better way than to reach for the reader on the table and continue reading her novel. All day he'd been waiting to get to it.

At first he thought he'd read only another chapter before calling it a night, but forty-five minutes later he was still immersed in her tale. He stopped a chapter before the end of the book. This story was more than a good read. Young-adult readers would find it sensational.

He could have finished it, but forced himself to save the last chapter for tomorrow night. When it was over, there wouldn't be anything else of hers to read. Except that wasn't true. Besides her school-magazine stories, she said she'd written other novels, but hadn't finished them. They were probably in storage. He planned to help her dig them out.

More than ever he understood why Roseanne had begged her to do another story. She'd wanted Lacey to write a sequel. Chaz would read it with equal enjoyment. There wasn't anything about Lacey he didn't enjoy. Like her radio show, there ought to be a warning for simply being around her—If you have a tendency to suffer from heart failure, we advise that you proceed with care since we will not be held responsible.

He got up from the table feeling both drained and exhilarated in a way he couldn't describe. After using the guest bathroom to brush his teeth, he made certain everything was locked up before shutting off the lights.

A man could get used to evenings like this. After he got ready for bed, he lay down on top of the sleeping bag wearing the bottoms of his sweats. It was too warm to cover himself. The fragrant night air called to him. The only way this scenario could be improved was if someone were to join him. A someone who'd created a fantasy world he longed to live in with her while they made love for hour upon hour.

CHAZ LEFT THE CONDO AT quarter to seven the next morning. It was already warm. He'd listened to the weather forecast and found out the temperature would climb to the nineties before thunderstorms moved in later in the day.

He could see clouds starting to gather over the mountains. Maybe he'd be sleeping on the couch tonight. Driving out to the main street, he phoned Tom, who was doing surveillance in the van. "What have you got for me?"

"It's been quiet."

"Things will have to pop before long."

"Agreed. I'll bring the tape in when I'm off duty at three."

"Thanks, Tom."

After stopping by his place for a shower and change

of clothes, he caught up with his friends at the Cowboy Grub for breakfast. It wasn't far from the office. They often met there to kick back and talk shop.

This was one time he wanted some input, but he was late. When they saw him walking toward their table, Travis, a former Texas Ranger, motioned the waitress over for more coffee. "Roman told us you're working a stalking case."

"It's a beaut!" Chaz sat down.

Mitch, who'd been a federal marshal in Florida before moving to Salt Lake, pushed a plate of bacon and scrambled eggs toward Chaz. "He said your client is that radio sensation who does the UFO stuff. What's she like in person? A little wacko?"

"I know what you're thinking. It's the same thing I thought before I met her."

"*Before* being the operative word?" Mitch drawled. Both men smiled, waiting to hear what was coming.

"If you want to know the truth, Lacey Pomeroy is the personification of any man's fantasy." Her little three-year-old would grow up to be just as beautiful and charming.

"That's the trouble with the best-looking women," Travis grumbled. "There's always a catch. Does she really think the government has a couple of ETs hidden under lock and key at Area 51?"

Chaz couldn't help but chuckle. "No, but if it were true, I assume she'd want to be the first person to break the news to her listening audience. How's your latest case going?"

Mitch made a face. "I'd rather think about your new assignment than the mail-fraud business I'm working on."

Travis finished off his coffee. "I feel left out. Roman's going to assign me to a new one when I get to the office. Use us while you can, Mitch."

For the next while Mitch brought them up to speed. Then the topic switched to Chaz. "Any new leads yet?"

"Just theories. I'll find out more when I go to this UFO conference with her this weekend."

Both men grinned. "We might as well let you know Roman told us your news."

"What do you mean?"

"That you're engaged."

"Come on, guys. You do what you have to do."

Mitch burst into laughter. "You sly dog."

"She must be something." Travis's eyes danced. "I'm afraid everyone in the office has seen her picture on the radio station's Ionosphere website and is betting that she'll end up your wife. You could have saved yourself the trouble by marrying her instead."

"You're right," Chaz admitted, "but she's still in love with her dead husband's memory. That would have been pushing it."

"What are your theories so far?"

He eyed them more soberly. "She's a celebrity who's written a *New York Times* bestseller, and she has the fourth leading paranormal radio talk show in the country. Lacey has two best friends who date back to elementary school and go to those UFO conferences, too. With a track record like she has, envy and jealousy for her success could give them opportunity and strong motives to see her harmed."

"That's true." Mitch pursed his lips. "Over that many years in a friendship, you pick up a lot of baggage along the way, good and bad. Some you can't slough off."

"My thoughts exactly," Travis echoed.

"But it's early in my investigation. There's this guy named Ken she's known for six years who had a meltdown on the phone when she told him she was engaged. But I didn't sense built-up rage behind his reaction."

"Maybe not at her." Travis winked. "But if he shows up at that conference, watch your back."

The three of them chuckled while Chaz finished off his eggs and bacon with a Danish.

"What's the gender ratio in this group?" Travis asked.

"Seven men, five women." Chaz had their profiles memorized down to their ages. "All are successful and in some cases prominent. Some are married, others divorced or single. Some have children."

"You've got your work cut out for you, but with the list you've compiled so far, I'd still wager the culprit's someone who has known her through thick and thin," Mitch reaffirmed. Then his phone rang, and he answered it.

After he clicked off, he stood up. "I've got to run. Stay in touch, guys." He shot Chaz a wicked glance. "Don't get any permanent ideas about that engagement business. You'd break up our triumvirate. We can't let that happen." He threw some bills on the table and took off.

Trust Mitch to zero in on Chaz's private thoughts about Lacey. He wasn't known around the office as the bloodhound for nothing.

Travis checked his watch. "I'm going to be late for a meeting with Roman I can't miss." He pushed himself away from the table and got to his feet. "I'll buy tickets if you want to catch the soccer game at Rio Tinto on Thursday. Six o'clock. Real Salt Lake is playing Dallas."

That was why Travis was excited. Once a Texan, always a Texan.

"Count me in for three."

His eyes lit up. "Yeah?"

Chaz grinned. "Yeah. May the best team win. Thanks, Travis. Put your money away. I'll take care of breakfast. I owe you for last time."

Chaz watched his friend walk off, but his mind was focused on the very real possibility that one of Lacey's childhood friends wanted to injure her. Perhaps not physically. Mental torture could cause horrendous fear and grief.

Why not use fear to force her to give up her radio show so she would disappear from the public eye for good? What better way to pay Lacey out for imagined sins.

The latest statistics proved that less than half the female stalking victims were directly threatened by their stalkers. Instead they were bombarded with threatening phone calls and letters.

He knew for a fact that more often than not female stalkers targeted professional contacts they hated or envied and were less likely to harass strangers than men. Female stalkers were also more likely to pursue victims they knew, who were of the same gender.

Chaz had already ruled out a lot of people on her list who didn't fit the profile, but Lacey's best friends *did*. The harassment had started at Ted Pomeroy's funeral when she would be her most vulnerable. It seemed his death had triggered the beginning of long-awaited plans of torture.

"More coffee?"

"No, thank you."

He paid the waitress, then left the restaurant. Once he reached the office, he had more research to do and planned to pore over the latest surveillance tapes before going back to Lacey's home. His pulse picked up speed just thinking about seeing her and Abby.

"Mommy! That's Chaz!"

As Lacey was removing her daughter from the car seat, he walked up to them dressed in tan chinos and a white polo.

It certainly was.

The moment she saw him, she felt that weakness in her legs again. They both must have pulled into their parking spaces at the same time. "Hi!"

The green flecks in his irises seemed to be more intense all of a sudden. "I'd say this was perfect timing." His gaze looked alive before it swerved to Abby. Lacey had just put her down so she could walk. The three of them headed for the stairs of the condo. Chaz gave her his full attention. "How's the butterfly princess?"

"I went to the libary."

The way his lips twitched at her daughter's mispronunciation caused Lacey's heart to kick. "Did you find a book you liked?"

She nodded. *"Pooh Bear and the BEES."*

He shared a smiling glance with Lacey, recognizing her daughter wasn't over the bee incident yet. "Did you bring it home?"

"Yes."

"Will you read it to me?" Chaz asked.

"No. Peach."

"Who's Peach?"

Lacey opened the door to her condo and they went inside. "Today my daughter is Peach, her favorite starfish from the movie *Finding Nemo*. She'll look at the pictures and tell you her own version of the story."

His eyes held a gleam. "We know where she gets her creativity from."

"But we don't know if she'll have an interest in UFOs. When she grows up, it will be just my luck if she writes a book denouncing me as a fraud."

She loved his rich male laughter. Abby didn't know the reason for it, but she laughed, too.

"Come on, honey. I'll warm up your mac and cheese. Would you like some, too, Chaz?"

"No, thank you. I had a late breakfast with some colleagues."

"I see. Then how about coffee? Lemonade?"

"In this heat, lemonade sounds good."

Abby climbed onto one of the dining room chairs with her Pooh book. She didn't like sitting in her high chair anymore, so Lacey had given it to the couple living in the unit below hers. They had a two-year-old and a new baby. Abby's high chair had been a welcome gift.

Chaz took a seat next to Abby. While he listened to her quaint version of the story complete with sound effects, Lacey served up lunch with some fruit, milk and lemonade. He dared Abby to eat her apple slices. She did, then he ate one, and they entertained each other eating up all the fruit with Abby laughing hilariously. For a man who'd never had children, Chaz was a natural with her.

In the midst of the laughter, the doorbell rang. Chaz shot her a glance. "Are you expecting anyone?"

"No."

"Go ahead and get it."

Lacey wiped her mouth on a napkin and got up from the table. When she opened the door, there was her striking friend whose black hair had been cut in a Cleopatra style for the play she'd been in at Pioneer Memorial Theater.

"Brenda—" Her voice caught. They'd known each other since third grade, but the terrorizing phone calls had turned her life inside out and she couldn't act natural with her friend.

"I know you weren't expecting me, but I had to come. Is it true you're engaged?"

"Guilty as charged." In the background she could almost hear Chaz telling her not to let on anything was wrong. "Come on in."

Once inside, her friend's brown eyes caught sight of the engagement ring. "You really are engaged!" She grabbed hold of Lacey's hand and studied it for a moment. "It's beautiful! Ken called me this morning and told me. I simply couldn't believe it!" She gave Lacey a warmhearted hug. "I'm so happy for you, I can't stand it. When did all this happen?"

Lacey would have answered, but Chaz came into the living room with Abby, who ran straight for Brenda. They gave each other a big hug before the little girl suddenly darted out of sight.

"Brenda Nichols, I'd like you to meet Chaz Roylance. I've told him our friendship goes back to childhood. He knows about you and your marvelous acting career."

"I'm pleased to meet you, Brenda." He shook her hand.

"She's just finished doing Shaw's *Caesar and Cleopatra*," Lacey explained.

"I'm impressed."

Brenda's gaze had been fastened on Chaz. There was a lot to take in. All of him was beyond attractive. After a minute she turned to Lacey. "Poor Ken. He never stood a chance anyway, and now...this." Her arms flew toward Chaz in a dramatic gesture.

That was the icebreaker for Lacey, who laughed out loud. "Poor Ken is right. How come you didn't tell me he wanted to go out with me?"

"Lacey..." She made a funny face. "How can you ask me that? Every time I bring up the subject of a man who'd like to meet you, you ask me to leave it alone and don't want to hear it. I knew you'd never had an interest in Ken, so I decided to stay quiet."

"Sorry I've been so difficult."

"I understand. Months ago I tried to put him off the idea of approaching you. But I didn't know about *this* man. Ken really took the news hard. If he comes to the conference this weekend, he'll probably wish he hadn't." She flashed Chaz a broad smile he reciprocated.

"Look!" Abby ran up to Brenda. She was hugging Chaz's present.

"Well, well. Diamonds and nesting dolls. I can see there's been a lot of excitement going on in *this* house."

Abby couldn't get the top open. She handed it to Chaz to help her. He undid it and soon she'd pulled all the dolls apart and had put everything on the couch.

"Here's the teeny baby." She handed it to Brenda to look at.

"Oh. She *is* teeny."

"Come on, honey." Lacey gathered her daughter. "It's time for your nap. Tell everyone you'll see them later."

"Okay. Bye, Chaz. Bye, Brenda." She took the baby with her.

Lacey sent Chaz a private glance. "I won't be long."

"Take your time. I want to get to know the friend who went out to the Great Salt Lake with you looking for meteors through a telescope."

Brenda's wide mouth broke into a grin. "I'm afraid my curiosity over you is even greater than yours about me. *I* want to hear the details of how you two met and how long this has been going on behind my back. This is an even bigger secret than her famous novel she never told anyone about!"

With her heart pounding until she felt sick, Lacey left to put her daughter down. When she returned to the living room ten minutes later, she found the two of them standing at the front door. He was telling her about his intention to start up a landscaping business.

Chaz saw her. "Brenda has to leave." To her shock, Chaz motioned her over and put his arm around her shoulders, drawing her close. Her breath caught in reaction to the first physical demonstration of affection from him. Heat stormed her face. Not only because he'd caught her by surprise, but because she liked being in his arms and wished it weren't an act.

"Brenda has agreed to let me sit with you during the

flight down. That's a real friend for you." He kissed her hot cheek.

Brenda put a hand on Lacey's arm. "I told him I wouldn't tell anyone else about your engagement. You can surprise everyone at the conference yourself. It'll be bigger news than a new UFO sighting." That drew a chuckle from Chaz.

"Unless Ken has already said something," Lacey murmured.

"I doubt it. He was pretty broken up."

"I didn't mean to hurt him."

"Of course not, but he obviously thought you knew how he felt. Maybe he's obtuse and that's what went wrong in his marriage. Anyway I told him you've always operated on a different wavelength so he shouldn't take it personally. But enough of that. I've got to run. I'll see you both on Friday morning at the airport. Congratulations again."

When she'd let Brenda out and closed the door, she found Chaz staring intently at her. "Was the Brenda I just met the Brenda you've always known?"

"Yes. If she's my stalker, she's the greatest actress alive, but then acting is her profession."

"You did a superb job yourself. If she's the culprit, then she left disappointed because you gave nothing of your terror away."

"I don't know how long I can keep this up."

His black brows furrowed. "Why? What is it?"

"Oh, just something she said. I would never have picked up on it if there were no stalker in my life. I've become paranoid."

"Like what?"

"She said I operated on a different wavelength.

We've been close for so many years, her comment came as a surprise because I don't know how she meant it. But I *do* know one thing no matter what. I love Brenda. She couldn't be the stalker, Chaz."

"Is it like her to just drop in on you?"

"When we were teenagers, yes, but since our marriages, she's always phoned me first and I, her."

"Ken's call caused her to do something out of the ordinary. In time we'll see if your friend has claws."

"I don't believe it." But a shudder racked her body anyway.

"Have you brought in the mail yet?"

She shook her head. "I'll get it now. Then I need to do some work before tonight's radio program."

"Is there anything I can do to help?"

A wry smile broke out on her face. "Not unless you want to read the book on Sasquatch I brought home from the library. The author is going to phone in tonight and be a guest. I need to read through it again. Especially the parts where he believes Sasquatch is one of the beings from another planet brought here as an experiment to see how they adapt."

"I'm looking forward to listening to the program."

His words said one thing, but the way he was looking at her was saying something else. Her bones had turned to water. Lacey could still feel the weight of his strong arm around her shoulders. He'd played the part of her fiancé just right. So right, she could almost believe they were really engaged. She hated that she felt so breathless.

"I'll be back in a minute."

She grabbed the keys from her purse and hurried outside to the mailbox. The usual stack of stuff was in there. Lots of brochures from scientific institutes and publishers of UFO fiction, a new catalogue of DVDs from Sinister Cinema where she'd ordered her Buck Rogers series. In the back was a package of vintage time-travel books.

When she returned, Chaz took the bundle from her and went into the family room to sort it out on the table. He went through the mail methodically. "The post office must know you well."

Lacey sat across from him. "I'm afraid so. I've been collecting paranormal material for a long time. One day years from now, I'm going to open my own sci-fi shop where people can browse and listen to old recordings, watch old videos and find books that have been out of print for years."

"It'll be a huge hit with all your fans."

"Right now it's just a dream. I've been looking into ways of preserving everything, but unfortunately today's methods are already obsolete. It's almost impossible to know where to start."

"But you'll try," he teased. "Here's a letter to you from the Albuquerque UFO Seminar Committee."

"Oh, good. After I got their first mailing a month ago, it occurred to me they didn't have Ed Margolitz on the docket to speak. I emailed them to find out why." She opened the creased envelope. "I hope this says he's going to be there."

"Will you shoot me if I ask you who he is?"

She laughed. "No. He's renowned for being the foremost authority on government conspiracies concerning UFOs." But when she unfolded the letter, there was nothing on the paper but two sentences typed in caps.

YOU'RE GOING TO BURN UP WHEN YOU
REACH ALBUQUERQUE. THAT'S NOTHING
COMPARED TO WHAT WILL HAPPEN TO
YOUR FREAKIN' DAUGHTER.

Chapter Six

When Chaz saw the blood drain from her face, he sprang from the chair and came around to read the letter himself. His torso brushed against her hair, sending a shock wave through his body.

"Don't touch the letter or the envelope, Lacey. Do you have any plastic bags? You know the kind."

She nodded and got up to find him some.

"I need tweezers if you have any."

"There's a pair in my bathroom." She returned with them seconds later.

He used them to carefully fold the paper over and place it in one bag. In the other, he slid the envelope. It had been postmarked last Friday from Albuquerque. "You told me the note you found on the windshield a year ago was done on white paper in caps." The author had used the word *freakin'* in other threats, as well. "This establishes a positive link between both time frames." His hunch had been right.

"Then it means I've been watched for a year now." Her voice shook.

"One way or another." Chaz clenched his teeth. "It's going to end soon." He needed to find the person responsible for causing so much chaos and pain in Lacey's life.

"Who's your contact on this committee? I'll need an address and phone number, too."

She looked up the information on her laptop and wrote it on a piece of paper. "How could he or she be in so many places?" she asked.

"Give me time and we'll get the culprit."

She nodded and handed him the paper.

"Thank you. When is your mail usually delivered?"

"Around one."

If Brenda was the stalker, then her unexpected visit might have been timed to see the state Lacey was in after opening her mail. Using Ken's phone call as the reason for dropping by would be a clever move on her part.

He wanted to take a look at today's surveillance tape. It would show the mailman filling the boxes. How soon after he'd left had Brenda arrived at the condo? Had she been out in her car waiting?

"I'm going to drop these off at the crime lab." Maybe there were no fingerprints for them to lift, but it was worth a try.

"What are you thinking, Chaz?"

"I'll tell you later." He squeezed her hand before he realized she might see the gesture as stepping over the line. He'd done it automatically. "Hang in there. You're doing brilliantly."

When he'd left the condo and reached his car, he phoned Tom. "How soon will your relief be here?"

"Half an hour."

"Come straight to the office. I need to analyze today's tape ASAP."

After going to the forensics lab downtown, he headed for work. On his way back to the office, his phone rang. He saw the caller ID and picked up. "Lacey?"

"I—I was just checking my email and there was another death threat."

"Read it to me."

"'Beware, you freakin' bitch.'" Her voice trembled. "'Life has been too easy for you, but aliens are going to take care of you and there's nothing your fiancé can do about it.'"

Though he knew it had terrified her, this couldn't be better news. "I had a hunch the engagement was going to be the catalyst to make things come to a head sooner."

"But only a few people know about it."

"Ken's had time to spread the word."

"Oh, Chaz—I'm scared."

"I know, but this is simply more of the same thing. We're getting closer. Don't forget. You've got protection right outside your door. Do you want me to phone your mother and ask her to come over?"

"No. Now that I've talked to you, I'm okay. Thanks."

"Call me anytime, Lacey, and I mean *anytime*."

"I will. Talk to you later."

He clicked off and parked behind the office. After hurrying inside, he found Roman testing out a new monitoring device his brother's spy-technology company had invented. Chaz knocked on the open door. His boss looked up. "Come on in. How's the stalking case coming?"

"Things have started to heat up since the word got out we're engaged. Lacey received a new death threat by email a little while ago." The stalker was clearly

someone from her core group to have heard the news
so quickly. "I need your help."

"Name it."

"It will require the authority to look through the records of the Albuquerque UFO Seminar Committee.
The records are probably located in someone's home.
This is Lacey's contact." He put the paper she'd given
him on Roman's desk.

For the next few minutes he went over the details of
the case. "The stalker got hold of their official envelope, or had one made up to look exactly like it. I want
to go through their phone bills, email and check dates
and times of their mailings.

"I need to know if they have a lot of envelopes on
hand they use from year to year. Do they print their
own or use a printing service? Who has access to the
supplies, one person or several? In the meantime the
crime lab will call and tell me what they find out about
the note. I'm hoping for a fingerprint, anything they can
find."

"I'll talk to Chief Mahoney and see what strings he
can pull for us with the Albuquerque Police Department."

"Thanks, Roman."

Chaz went back to his office to watch the tape Tom
had brought in. It had filmed the mailman pulling up
in his minivan at ten to one. Brenda got there at quarter
after two. She wouldn't have known when Lacey went
out for the mail, but she could have been on a fishing
expedition all the same.

Before Chaz knew it, the day was gone. Hungry for
dinner, he picked up some pizza with salad and drinks

to go before heading to Lacey's condo. He bought some cinnamon bread sticks, too. Abby might like those.

Adam had parked his surveillance van in the guest area. His presence gave Chaz peace of mind and was helping Lacey get through this without falling apart.

Chaz pulled into the stall he used. After grabbing his backpack, he hurried up the stairs with the food, eager to be with her and Abby. Hopefully he'd get some time alone with Lacey after the program. The predicted storm front had moved in. Gusting winds were so strong that when he unlocked the door, it blew open to reveal a woman standing in the living room.

As he stepped inside and shut it, he didn't know who looked more surprised, he or Lacey's sister. He knew her from the yearbook and photographs placed around the living room, plus the photo Lacey had given him to scan.

"Sorry if I startled you, Ruth. I'm Chaz Roylance. Nice to meet you." He shook her hand.

Beneath shoulder-length strawberry-blond hair, her sky-blue eyes swept over him. "You look like one of the studs I saw on a P.I. show last month."

That was direct. "Hopefully it won't be too long before I catch Lacey's stalker."

"It's probably a guy she never noticed and the rejection crushed him. Lacey has a tendency to do that. Just cut the dude's heart out."

Chaz was glad Lacey had told him about her sister's unique personality. "Then again it could be a woman who'd been in love with Ted and couldn't take it when he married Lacey."

She put her hands on her hips. "Then she told you about Shelley."

Shelley? "No. I was only throwing out another possible scenario."

"You must be psychic."

"Why do you say that?"

"Because this one was obsessed with Ted and continued to be up to the time he died."

Chaz weighed her comment before he said, "I'll ask her about it. Excuse me while I put this food on the dining room table."

Ruth followed him into the family room. Unlike Lacey, she was blunt and very much aware of herself. He'd met attractive women with an attitude who liked to challenge a man on a first meeting. She was one of them, standing there in a light green tank top and jeans.

He judged her to be a couple of inches taller than Lacey, who stood five foot five. Of the two, Lacey was the more curvaceous. Ruth was good-looking, but compared to her sister... In truth he couldn't think of another woman who came close to possessing Lacey's stunning attributes.

"Do you like your job?"

What a question. He lowered his backpack to the floor. "I do. Every case is different."

"I'd be curious to know what the odds are of you catching this pathetic person."

"A hundred percent."

She smiled. "Wow. A man totally sure of himself. Most guys like to *pretend* they are."

"So do most women. Where your sister's and Abby's lives are concerned, I'm deadly earnest about my job."

To his surprise she gave a little mock shiver. "You've convinced me." She was flirting with him. There was no law against it. Ruth was single. Lacey would have told her he was a widower.

But Ruth had several strikes against her. Besides the fact that she was Lacey's sister, she didn't appeal to him. Since he'd see her coming and going, he needed to strike the right balance with her while he was doing his investigation in order not to offend her.

"Is your sister putting Abby down?"

"Not yet. She's getting ready to go to work."

"Then I'm not too late. I brought treats for them."

"Abby's watching *Dora*."

"Is that a film?"

"It's a children's program," Lacey answered, having just come in from the living room. "I thought I heard a voice, but Abby picked up on it first. She said, 'Mommy, that's Chaz!'"

He liked hearing that.

Lacey's little girl was right behind her, hugging her toy frog. When she saw Chaz, she made a happy sound and ran over to him in her pink princess jammies. Without conscious thought, he swept her up in his arms. She smelled sweet like her mother. "Where are your butterfly wings?"

"I can't find them."

He chuckled. "Would you like a surprise?"

Lacey's gaze met his head-on. "You're spoiling her."

"Am I bad?" He grinned.

She smiled back. "Yes, you are."

"Has she had dinner?"

"Luckily, yes."

"What's my surprise?" Abby wanted to know.

He put her down and opened the box of warm cinnamon bread sticks. "Go ahead and try one."

She reached carefully for one, looked at it for a minute, then took an experimental bite. "Mmm." Her eyes lit up. She took another bite and finished the bread stick off in no time. "Thanks."

He eyed Lacey, who'd put on a silky peach blouse with a beige wraparound skirt. With her coloring and figure, she looked sensational.

"There's food for all of us, Lacey."

"I didn't realize you'd be bringing dinner home. That's very thoughtful. I hate not being able to join you, but I had to eat early because I need to get down to the station and set things up for tonight's guest. Come on, Abby. Now that you've had your treat and seen Chaz, it's time for bed. Let's brush your teeth."

"Come on, Chaz." Abby pulled on his leg.

"No, honey," Lacey said. "He has to eat his dinner. Say good-night."

"Okay. Good night, Chaz. Good night, Auntie Ruth."

"Get a good sleep."

When they disappeared, Chaz turned to her. "Have you eaten, too?"

"No. I barely got here before you blew in."

He remembered unlocking the door before the wind blew it wide open. "So I did," he said with a chuckle, still aware of the weather getting nastier out there. He didn't like the idea of Lacey driving to work in it. "Please join me, then. I don't want this food to go to waste. It's never as good the next day."

"You're right. Thanks. This beats peanut butter and jelly." She sat down opposite him and they began to eat. "Lacey told me about the latest threats. She's asking for it by doing the talk show here. I think she's a fool."

He detected impatience in her tone. "People have to work."

"She doesn't have to do this kind. It's put Mom out. You would have thought she'd have given it up after she got the first threat down in Long Beach. But she loves the limelight too much to worry about Abby, who dreads it every time she leaves for work. Dad would turn over in his grave."

"Your father wouldn't approve of her radio show?"

"Hardly," she muttered. "He was the most private man I ever knew. I wish he were still alive. Life would be very different if he hadn't died."

"In what way?"

She darted him a chilly glance. "Lots of ways that are none of your business, even if you are a P.I." Then she smiled. "You've got enough on your plate dealing with Lacey's problem. She's been a mess without Dad."

Not Ted?

Ruth puzzled him. Her mind really wasn't on Lacey's stalker. In fact, he felt a disconnect here that wasn't normal. Finding the culprit was uppermost in the minds of most family members of the victim, but Ruth was focused on herself. In less than a minute her mood had changed from being accusatory to angry to introspective and defensive. It all seemed to be tied up in thoughts about her and her father. He could hardly keep up.

"Even so I find your sister to be a strong woman."

"That's because *you've* been hired." Her eyes lingered on him.

"No, she has inner resources and a little charmer who needs her. That helps her cope. You and your mother have the same kind of strength, otherwise you wouldn't carry on as you do in the face of this stalker. I admire you for coming over here to tend Abby."

"Lacey said you've put her under constant protective surveillance. Knowing that, it isn't hard for me to stay here. The stalker isn't after me and I need the money."

The coldness of her comment didn't sit well with him. "It's still a frightening proposition and takes courage, even if you *are* a gutsy pilot."

Her brows went up as if she was surprised he knew about her job. "An unemployed one at the moment."

"I hope that changes for you soon. In the meantime I know Lacey's grateful you're able to be here for Abby."

As he finished off another piece of pizza, Lacey came back into the family room. "Abby's asleep. Goodbye, you two. I'll be home at twelve-thirty."

Chaz got up from the table. "There's going to be a downpour pretty soon. Since Ruth is here, I'll drive you to the station and watch you in action."

"You don't need to do that."

He put his hands on his hips. "It's part of what I do." If she knew the strength of his feelings, she'd probably run a mile.

Her eyes rounded. "All right, then." She looked at her sister. "Thanks for watching Abby. I couldn't do this without you."

Ruth didn't say anything. After what she'd shared with Chaz, he deduced that tending Abby helped pay a few bills but wasn't a labor of love on her part.

Chaz brought his bedding into the kitchen from the deck and locked the sliding door. After picking up his backpack, he headed for the front door. Lacey followed. They hurried down to his car where he helped her inside. Once he'd stowed his pack in the trunk, he got in behind the wheel.

The second he started the engine, the rain descended in a torrent accompanied by lightning and thunder. Lacey's eyes flicked to his. "We made it to the car just in time. I'm glad you're driving me tonight," she whispered.

He struggled to catch his breath. "So am I. This hasn't been an easy day for you and now this storm. It'll be fun to sit in on your show."

"I'm afraid you'll die of boredom."

"Want to bet? Do you have that library book with you?"

"It's in my bag, but thanks for reminding me. I've tucked notes all the way through to help me remember the questions I need to ask my guest."

"I have no doubt you could wing it if you had to. When we arrive at the station, go ahead and introduce me as your fiancé." Being her fiancé sounded right to him and was sounding more right all the time. The line he wasn't supposed to cross had disappeared.

"It'll be a huge surprise to everyone there."

"I think it surprised your sister." He was still trying to sort out his impression of Ruth, who'd come off sounding narcissistic.

"Except that she knows the reason for it and she likes you."

His hands tightened on the steering wheel. Had Lacey said that to remind him their engagement was only temporary? The heat of frustration permeated his body. If she was going to start playing Cupid, he had news for her. "What makes you say that?"

"She would have gone to her room otherwise."

"It was the food. She was hungry."

NO. IT WAS MUCH MORE THAN that. Ruth was interested.

Lacey had seen the deflated look on her face when Chaz insisted on driving Lacey to the station. With the slightest encouragement from him, her sister would go in pursuit. Ruth had probably never met a man who was larger than life before.

If Lacey was being honest with herself, neither had she.... When she'd awakened this morning, her first thought had been of Chaz. She had to face the fact that he'd become very important to her and she wanted him to feel the same way. Abby was already crazy about him.

"Have you ever been to a soccer game, Lacey?"

The subject was totally unexpected. She darted him a curious glance. "No."

"Would you like to see one?"

"Probably about as much as you wanted to read a young-adult fantasy. Both activities have to be acquired tastes, but since it's *you* inviting me..."

An unmistakable gleam of satisfaction entered his eyes, thrilling her. "We need a break from the stress. I have another ticket for Abby. Might as well get her started early."

A real family activity. She hadn't done anything like it for over a year and had trouble hiding her excitement. "I take it you love soccer."

"I'll always love American football, but I've been around the world with the SEALs, and soccer's the only game in town. It's on Thursday at Rio Tinto Stadium. Starts at six. Real Salt Lake is playing Dallas. If Abby gets too restless, we'll leave early. We can still get you to the radio station on time for your program."

"Abby and I would love to go. That part of my education has been neglected too long. Thank you."

Though some maniac was after her, Chaz had burst into her life with all the power and speed of a stargrazer. He'd brought an energy foreign to her. She couldn't get enough of it. *Of him.* She wanted to go with him, be with him.

When she'd seen the way Ruth had looked at him back at the condo, she'd almost warned her sister that Chaz was off-limits. It was a primitive emotion, one that really surprised Lacey because she'd never known such a possessive feeling before. She'd never been a jealous person, but the thought of him being with anyone else…

"We've arrived." His deep voice broke her train of thought. "While there's a lull in the storm, let's make a dash for it."

"I'm afraid we don't have a choice, anyway. My guest for the show is waiting for a phone call."

He came around to her side and helped her out of his Forerunner. Together they ran for the door. It hadn't been much of a lull. Once inside the building, they shook off the rain and smiled at each other.

Chaz was so handsome. "There you are, looking like the underwater SEAL you used to be, while I…well, let's just say this is why I don't do a TV show."

His hazel eyes reflected pleasure as they roamed over her hair and features. "You're beautiful wet or dry."

The huskiness in his tone sent scorching heat to her face. She murmured a thank-you and headed down the hall, her pulse racing. She needed to let Stewart know she was there.

Kurt was in the broadcast room doing his show. All seemed well until she saw her normally happy intern. When she appeared in his doorway, she caught sight of him standing at his desk looking anxious and unnerved. He was on the phone with Barry because she heard him say the producer's name. When he saw her, he dangled a fax in front of her.

It proved one thing. Stewart wasn't her stalker. There was no way he could fake a demeanor like that or his loss of color.

Before she could blink, Chaz stepped forward and took the fax from him. Knowing she'd just received another threat, she would probably have suffered an anxiety attack if Chaz hadn't brought her to the station. He was always so calm.

Instead of showing it to her, he said, "Go ahead and make that long-distance call in your office. I'll join you in a minute."

Thankful for Chaz, she went through to her office. During the conversation with her guest, she had to concentrate, but it was hard to do when she could see into Stewart's office. The two men talked the whole time she was on the phone.

Once she got off, she made her way to the broadcast booth Kurt had just vacated. Soon she was on the air. The Sasquatch topic had the lines jammed with callers. For the next three hours, Lacey was forced into the paranormal world she loved.

Chaz stayed in Stewart's office. Every once in a while he caught her eye. The warmth in his expression was the only thing that kept her going. Somehow she made it through the program. When she was off the air, he came to the door of the booth to hustle her out of the building.

They swept past the night watchman, trying to avoid the puddles left by the cloudburst. It had passed over, but you could still hear rumblings to the south. He helped her into his car.

On the drive home he glanced over at her. "That was a great show. You're a real star, Lacey. I don't mean in the celebrity sense, though you are that. I'm talking about the professional way you handle yourself in the face of terror."

"You know very well it's a facade." She rubbed her arms. "What did the fax say?"

"The same kind of threat. Barry told Stewart he'd handle it and asked him not to discuss the incident with anyone. I told him that as your fiancé, I won't let anything happen to you. It's clear he was genuinely horrified by the fax."

"How cruel for this to affect his work, too."

"If anything, he's worried for you. While you were doing your show, I traced the fax back to the Cowboy Mart in Evanston, Wyoming. They provide a customer fax service. Because of privacy issues, they couldn't tell me who sent it. Even if I'd had access, it wouldn't be the real name of your stalker."

Lacey shifted several times. "When did it come through to the station?"

"Three o'clock this afternoon."

She groaned. "How can the threats come from so many places almost at the same time?"

"This person is probably getting help."

"Two people?" she cried in panic.

"It's only a possibility. Let me worry about it."

"Every time a new threat comes, it wears me down a little more."

"That's the stalker's purpose, but you're not going to cave. Stewart told me the station has never had more callers for your show. He has nothing but praise for you and sent his congratulations on our engagement."

Her hand shook slightly before smoothing some hair away from her temple. "About the engagement—"

"It's working like a charm," he broke in. "Your stalker is losing control of the situation and it's showing."

Lacey's racing heart was proof that her feelings for him were also getting out of control.

The flash from the fake diamonds in the ring reminded her of the dangerous game she and Chaz were playing.

When he caught the person or persons menacing her—and he would, she had no doubt of that—she'd have to give the ring back. Then he'd be out of her life and on to a new case that had nothing to do with her.

Better get used to the idea, Lacey. Better not get too comfortable. Better focus.

Chapter Seven

Chaz felt disappointment when he walked into the condo with Lacey and saw that Ruth was still up watching TV in the family room. He'd hoped for a few more minutes of privacy with Lacey before they said goodnight.

"Hi," Ruth called out from the couch.

"Hi," Lacey said in a quieter voice. Chaz wondered if she was also disappointed Ruth was still up. "How did it go tonight?"

"Abby never wakes up. You had a call from Jenny. When I saw her caller ID, I picked up and caught her so she wouldn't have to leave a message."

"Did she say what she wanted?"

Chaz listened to them talk as he put his backpack next to his bedding, which was resting against the sliding door to the deck.

"She was ticked off that she had to hear about your engagement from someone else. You're supposed to phone her in the morning."

"I'll call her." Lacey's gaze swerved to Chaz, who by now had gone to the sink for a glass of water. "I guess Ken was more upset than I thought."

"Or maybe Brenda couldn't hold back from telling the news to her other best friend," he murmured.

Ruth turned off the TV and came into the kitchen. "Ken? Isn't he the rocket scientist?"

"No. That's Derrick. Ken's the biochemist."

"Why would he be upset?"

"He called the other night to ask me to dinner after the seminar on Saturday. I told him I couldn't because I just got engaged."

Ruth eyed her speculatively. "Maybe he's the one who's been harassing you." Her gaze flicked to Chaz. "What do *you* think?"

"The man is on my list of suspects."

She lounged against the counter in a pose meant to be provocative. "Is it a long one?"

"Until I find your sister's stalker, everyone is on it."

"I guess that includes *moi.*"

"Don't ever say that!" Lacey rushed over to hug her. "Not even in jest. Thanks for tending Abby. I don't know what I'd do without you and Mom."

"Or your fiancé?" Ruth smiled at him over Lacey's shoulder.

Her younger sister had what he would politely describe as a cheeky attitude. It was in her makeup to push an issue or a man to the edge. The woman didn't recognize boundaries. Maybe he was wrong, but he suspected she'd stayed up late in the hope of talking to him once Lacey had said good-night.

"Abby will be up early. I don't know about you, Ruth, but I'm exhausted and am going to bed." Lacey turned to Chaz. "I'm afraid the deck might be too wet for you tonight. The family room is all yours."

"Thanks. Good night, you two." He purposely included Ruth in his glance. "I'll lock up and turn off lights."

Glad to see Ruth leave with Lacey, Chaz checked the deck. The rain had lowered the temperature to the seventies. Perfect for sleeping and the boards were dry enough. He preferred staying outside.

Perhaps it wasn't fair of him, but he wouldn't put it past Ruth to saunter into the family room early in the morning on some pretext of getting a bite to eat or a drink. Chaz didn't want to be caught lying there and be forced to talk to her. And he certainly didn't want Lacey to get the wrong idea if she saw them together.

He felt sure Ruth wouldn't have any qualms about opening the door to the deck tomorrow just to say good morning if it were just the two of them, but she might think twice about it with Lacey in the house. How ironic that he was staying here to protect Lacey, yet he found *himself* needing to be cautious when it came to Ruth.

Chaz had been around women like her before. Lacey hadn't needed to tell him her sister liked men.

Checking to be sure the front door was locked, he turned out the lights and got ready for bed. Once *inside* his sleeping bag for a change, his thoughts remained on Lacey and her sister. What was it he'd studied about the sibling bond? It was life's longest relationship, outlasting parents, spouses, even best friends.

He hadn't grown up with siblings, but knew they weren't minor players on the stage of life. They went through distinctive emotional periods. Besides rivalry, they experienced longing, hero worship, shame, envy, jealousy, tenderness and feelings of obligation.

One comment from a prominent psychologist claimed

that a sibling could be your sweetest companion or your worst enemy.

Your worst enemy.

Ruth's own comment about being on the suspect list—a comment that had upset Lacey—was troubling him. When he thought about it, except for Mrs. Garvey, Lacey's longest relationship had been with her sister. Longer than her association with Brenda and Jenny.

Curious to know more about her, he phoned Lon, one of his backup crew.

"Chaz? What's up?"

"Sorry to wake you. Can you be at Lacey's place by six in the morning?"

"Sure."

"Tom will be on duty to watch her and Abby. I need you to keep an eye on her sister, Ruth. You have a picture of her. Strawberry-blond shoulder-length hair, five foot seven. She drives a red 2009 Mazda with Idaho plates. Check on her registration and do a police background check. If she leaves the condo in the morning, go wherever she goes and check in with me."

"Will do."

"Thanks, Lon."

Chaz had no idea how Ruth spent her time when she'd exhausted her job search for the day, but to do a thorough investigation, he had to find out. According to Lacey, her sister was out of work and looking for employment with an air cargo company. For the time being, Lacey didn't need to know he was having Ruth followed.

Lacey… If all went well tomorrow, he had plans for her and Abby.

The next morning he left Lacey's earlier than usual.

To his surprise, Lon rang him at eight while Chaz was leaving his own condo to drive to the office. He picked up. "Have you got something for me already?"

"Ms. Garvey is the owner of the Mazda. She's clean. No arrests, no warrants out on her. She left the condo at ten after six and stopped at a drive-thru for breakfast. I followed her to the small airport at Salt Lake International. She parked her car and walked over to one of the hangars to talk to a guy who looked to be in his late twenties. From there they got into a Cessna Skylane and took off, with him at the controls.

"I phoned Roman. He used his airport sources and learned they were headed for St. George, Utah. The pilot's name is Bruce Larson. His home base is Idaho Falls, Idaho."

Lacey had said she'd heard her sister talking to a Bruce on the phone. Obviously they'd met in Idaho. "You're the best, Lon."

"What do you want me to do now?"

"Nothing more at the moment. What's your schedule like tomorrow? Is one of the other guys using you?"

"No. I'm free."

"Unless you hear from me, plan to do the same thing in the morning, same time."

"Will do."

Chaz hung up, wondering what the pilot was doing at Salt Lake International. It cost money to fly all those places unless he was doing a cargo run. Were they lovers? Had Ruth gone along for the ride while she was waiting for a job offer to come through?

When he let himself into the office, Roman was in the back room drinking coffee. He flashed Chaz a smile. "You've been busy and keeping everyone else busy, too."

"Tell your wife I'm sorry I had to wake you so early with that phone call."

"Comrade," Roman said with his Russian accent, "that is the name of this *beezness*. She understands. Doing *beezness* for her was how we met."

Chaz couldn't help but chuckle. "Things are starting to happen."

Roman pointed at him. "That's because of you. Grab a cup of java and come into my office. I've got news from the crime lab about the envelope and note you took in for analysis. They sent a fax."

A few minutes later Chaz lifted his head from the paper. "Latent fingerprints weren't distinct, but they found two hairs in the envelope, one four inches long, the other seven."

Roman nodded. "Read on."

"'Test reveals the hairs are human, Caucasian, blond with traces of red pigment containing pheomelanin. The hairs have been treated. Blond hair can have almost any proportion of pheomelanin and eumelanin, but both only in small amounts. More pheomelanin creates a more golden-blond color, and more eumelanin creates an ash blond.'"

Chaz let out a whistle. "Whether male or female, whoever put the death threat in that envelope could be the stalker. The problem is, I don't know if the hairs were already inside it when the stalker got hold of it. What about the Albuquerque police, have they come up with anything?"

"Chief Mahoney said he'd get back to me when he's had word. If he hasn't called by this afternoon, I'll give him a ring. Obviously the information from the UFO committee is critical."

Chaz paced in front of Roman's desk, drinking his coffee. "Whoever put the note in the envelope probably used gloves, but they didn't notice that two hairs were either already in the envelope or fell into it as they worked."

"Every criminal makes a mistake somewhere," Roman muttered. "This may be the evidence you need to crack the case."

Adrenaline surged through Chaz's body. "Depending on what we learn from the Albuquerque police, the hair color could narrow the field by a huge margin." When he flew with Lacey to Albuquerque, he'd get a firsthand, up-close look at every blond man or woman in her group, including any on the UFO planning committee.

"I've got to go. Talk to you later, Roman."

On the way out to his car, he bumped into Travis. His friend pulled some tickets out of his pocket. "I got us good seats."

"Excellent." Chaz drew a few bills from his wallet to pay for them. "Who's coming?"

"Roman, Rand and Eric with their families, Mitch and I, Lisa and Jim. And you with your…" His eyes danced.

"The jury's out at the moment." Chaz couldn't solve this case fast enough. He wanted to be with her in a nonprofessional way. "Thanks for getting these. Why don't you surprise everyone and bring a date."

Travis paused in the doorway. "Your surprise is going to be enough for one night." He still hadn't gotten

over the loss of his wife, who'd been murdered in a re-
venge killing. Who could? "See you later."

THE SCREAMS COMING FROM the other part of the condo
had Lacey racing from the kitchen to reach her daughter. Abby came flying down the hall in hysterics.

"Honey—" She crushed her in her arms. "What's
wrong? Tell Mommy."

Her little girl actually shook and thrashed about, still
screaming so hard she couldn't talk.

"Abby, sweetheart—"

The next thing she knew Chaz's hard-muscled body
filled the hallway. She hadn't heard him come in.
"What's happened?"

At the sound of his deep voice, Abby turned her
tear-drenched, splotchy red face to him. "A big bee!"
She reached for him and buried her body against his
broad chest. He wrapped his strong arms around her
and rocked her while she sobbed.

When Lacey had recovered from her fright, plus
from the fact that her daughter had automatically
sought Chaz's protection, she said, "Where did you
see it?"

"I-in the w-window!" She half hiccuped the words,
pointing to her bedroom before she hid her face in
Chaz's neck once more.

"Mommy will get it."

"No!" Abby screamed again.

"Honey, I'm not scared of the bee. You stay with
Chaz."

Her daughter's cries followed Lacey into the bedroom. When she reached the locked window where
Abby had been arranging her nesting dolls along the

sill, she saw a wasp outside, climbing on the other side of the glass.

Though Lacey knew it couldn't hurt her, it was black, and the sight of it was a surprise to her, too. She could just imagine how terrifying it looked to Abby, who still wasn't over the fright from her bee sting.

She hurried back out of the room. Her eyes fused with Chaz's searching gaze before she reached for Abby. "That bee can't hurt you." She covered Abby's face and hair in kisses. "He's outside."

"No. He isn't!" she insisted.

"Yes. Chaz will go in the room first and show you. That mean old bee can't come in."

Abby practically strangled her as they followed him into the bedroom. "Chaz—" she spoke softly "—if we don't help her through this, she won't go to sleep in here. That would be another nightmare I don't want to live through."

"Message understood," he whispered back. "Yup. I can see him, Abby. He's outside the window, just like your mommy said. He can't come in, sweetheart. Do you know what I'm going to do?"

She was still trembling. "What?"

"I'm going outside to kill it. Do you want to watch?"

Abby clung tighter to Lacey. "Yes."

"Okay. Stay right where you are." His eyes flicked to Lacey's. "There's a ladder in the surveillance truck. See you in a minute."

They stayed right where they were. Abby kept her head burrowed against Lacey's chest. Before long, she saw Chaz at the window, former navy SEAL performing the kind of surgical maneuver his training had taught him. For a uniform, he wore a dark blue sport shirt and gray chinos. He had an incredible physique and was an eyeful in whatever he wore.

"Look at the window, Abby. There's Chaz. He's waving to you to come over."

"Where's the bee?" She probably didn't realize her right hand was pinching Lacey's arm.

"It's dead. He wants to show you. Shall we go see it?"

Slowly Abby nodded. Lacey took a few steps closer. Chaz's smiling face transformed him into the most attractive man she'd ever seen in her life.

"Hi, sweetheart." He held up a rag with the wasp lying on it. "See?" He picked it up and put it in his hand. "He's dead!"

Abby finally believed it and the tension went out of her body. "He won't come back?"

"Never!" Chaz promised her. "Shall we flush him down the toilet?"

"The toilet." She laughed hilariously.

"That's where we put all bad bees," he told her. "Do you want to watch?"

"Yes."

"Okay. Just a minute."

The hero of the hour returned before Lacey could blink. He went into the guest bathroom. Lacey stood by the door with Abby. "One, two, three." He let the wasp fall into the water, then he flushed it away before smiling at her. "He's all gone."

"Let me see." Abby got down and hugged his leg while she looked. "He's gone, Mommy," she said in her bright little voice.

Even though it was just a bee, the incident had caught Lacey with emotions that were already raw.

"Yes," she said in a tear-filled voice. "The mean old bee is gone." Her wet eyes lifted to their hero.

"Oh, Chaz…" Without conscious thought she took a step to hug him. She needed his solid warmth to work through the moment. "What would I have done if you hadn't been here?"

With his arms enveloping her, he crushed her against him. "You would have handled it like you've been doing since she was born, but I'm glad I was here. I've never been a parent, but when I heard her screaming, it terrified me and gave me a taste of what it would be like."

He kissed her hair and temple. "She's a priceless little thing. Though we haven't known each other very long, I love your daughter."

His admission tugged at her heart. "I love her, too. That's why I'm so grateful." Suddenly Lacey realized where they were and what she was doing. He'd done a lot more than help Abby through an emotional moment. He was saving Lacey's sanity. Embarrassed to have let her feelings explode on him like this, she eased out of his arms.

"Come on, honey." She reached for Abby's hand and walked her into the living room.

Chaz trailed them. "I have an idea. What do you say we go get lunch, and then play at the park. The temperature is up in the low eighties. Not a cloud in the sky. After last night's storm, it's perfect weather."

Lacey looked down at her daughter. "Do you want to go to the park with Chaz?"

"Yes." She clapped her hands.

He leaned over her. "Do you have a ball?"

Her nod caused her curls to bounce. "I'll get it." She ran out of the room.

They both watched her disappear. "Thanks to you, she's not afraid to go to her bedroom," Lacey said.

Chaz studied her upturned face. "To make certain this doesn't happen again soon, your landlord needs to be called. I saw some wasp nests beneath the eaves. They should be knocked down and sprayed."

"You're a lifesaver in more ways than one. I'll call his number right now and leave a message."

Abby came back as Lacey was hanging up the phone. She had her big-girl bag stuffed with some of her toys.

In a few minutes Lacey had collected a blanket and they left for the drive-thru where they could park beneath a covered area to eat. They agreed that if they didn't eat food at the park, maybe the bees would stay away.

Lacey drove her car because it had the car seat in the back. This was the first time she'd taken Chaz anywhere. So far he'd done everything for her. She loved the idea of being able to reciprocate.

After they'd eaten, she headed for the neighborhood park dotted with plenty of trees. They found shade on the grass next to the playground and set out a blanket. Lacey had brought some bottled water from the fridge.

Chaz watched as she put sunscreen on her and Abby. "Considering your gorgeous coloring, that's a good idea. The sun's hot out here."

She kissed Abby to hide her reaction to his choice of words. "We redheads have to be careful."

Her daughter found the ball in her bag and rolled it to Chaz. He rolled it back and a game was on. She would try to catch it before it whizzed past her. Abby was in heaven. So was Lacey. They took turns playing catch.

For a little while she could pretend nothing was wrong in her world.

Next, Abby wanted to swing. She pointed to the swing set. "Come on." With those fast legs of hers, she darted toward them. But the seats were too big and she had trouble getting in.

Chaz reached one and invited Lacey to sit on it. "I'll swing you both." He put Abby in her arms. "Ready?"

"Yes!" Abby squealed in delight.

He started out with care to make sure she was handling it, then he pushed a little harder. At one point the swing went high enough both Abby and Lacey cried out in excitement. Lacey could hear Chaz laughing behind them. When the swing went back to him that time, he caught them in his arms. "Got ya."

Abby giggled, waiting for him to let them go again. Lacey's heart was pounding out of control because Chaz's cheek was against hers. Being cocooned in his arms, her back was pressed into his chest where his heart beat just as hard as her own. It made her so aware of his masculinity, she felt desire, hot and unmistakable, curl through her body. She almost lost her breath. If he hadn't been holding on to them, she would have fallen.

He must have realized what was happening to her because he let them go gently, otherwise they would have gone flying. When the swing came to a stop, Abby wanted to go again, but Lacey needed to recover from being in Chaz's arms and stepped to the ground. She set Abby on her feet, as well.

Avoiding his eyes she said, "I'm thirsty. Shall we go get a drink?"

"Chaz, swing me!"

"Say please, Abby. Maybe he's thirsty, too."

"Please."

Without a word, he sat in the swing and put Abby on his lap. While he entertained her daughter, Lacey walked back to the blanket and sank down, still trembling from the experience. Not since Ted had she felt this alive.

She'd wanted Chaz to kiss her. Her face went hot because she knew he knew it. That's why he'd been so quiet.

It hadn't been a full week, yet already she couldn't imagine her life without him. Though a stalker was after her and her fear was very real, Chaz had taken away her terror. In its place something else was growing. She didn't dare put a name to it because once she did, she'd want it too much.

Just as she was thinking the sun was too hot, Chaz and Abby walked back to the blanket. "Here's your water, honey." She undid the cap.

Abby plopped down by her toy bag and reached for the water. Chaz lay down on his side and propped his head in order to drink his. What a beautiful man.... He was close enough Lacey could feel his warmth and breathe in the scent of the soap he'd used.

She felt his gaze travel over her body. She'd dressed in a simple cream top and jeans, but he clearly liked what he saw. "Did you get a chance to talk to your friend Jenny this morning?"

Though his eyes were on her, his mind was on her case. He could do two things at once. She had an almost impossible time focusing on anything but him. "I caught her before she left for the university."

"How did she find out about the engagement?"

"When she phoned Mom in an effort to find me, Mom told her."

"Was she happy for you?"

"Cautiously pleased. Her divorce has jaded her somewhat. She warned me it was awfully soon to jump into marriage again. Why be in a hurry for something that might not work out a second time?"

Chaz frowned. "She really was hurt."

"That's because her ex-husband had an affair on her."

"Did you see it coming?"

Lacey smoothed some hair out of her eyes. "No. I really liked Mark. They seemed to be crazy about each other. His infidelity came as a shock to everyone."

"I'm sorry for her."

"Me, too."

"Is she coming to Albuquerque?"

"Yes. I didn't realize her dad's going through chemo for prostate cancer. She's going to fly back here after the conference and stay with her parents for a couple of weeks. She wants to get together. That's why she called."

"Then I'll have an opportunity to meet her."

Lacey winced. "Jenny isn't the one, Chaz. I just know she isn't."

She jumped to her feet, hating the direction of their conversation. Here she'd had one of the most wonderful days she'd ever known, but the specter of the stalker tainted everything. "Come on, honey. It's time to go home for your nap. It's going to be a late one today."

While Chaz helped Abby put her toys back in the bag, Lacey threw the empty bottles in the recycle bin and folded up the blanket. When they got home, Abby had no qualms about going to her bedroom, but she wanted Chaz to stay with her until she fell asleep with her frog.

Lacey went into the family room and sat down in front of her laptop to plan out tonight's radio program. Before long Chaz joined her, wearing a sober expression. "I'm sorry to have upset you at the park."

Guilt swamped her. "Surely you know it wasn't you," she blurted. "How could I blame you for anything? We had a marvelous time today and it's obvious my daughter sees you as her champion. From the moment Barry hired you, you've saved me from going over the edge. I'd be an ungrateful wretch if I didn't tell you how thankful I am." *How crazy I am about you.*

"I think you've said it a dozen times already." He picked up the reader from the table. "I promised Abby I'd be here when she wakes up. She wants me to inspect the window for bees."

Lacey shook her head. "I'm sorry. The poor little thing really is terrified of insects. I hope it's a passing phase."

"I'm sure it is. While she's asleep, I'm headed for the deck where I can stretch out and finish your book. It's part of my investigation. I've been saving the last chapter to read when I could relax. If you want, why don't you bring your laptop and join me."

What?

"When you're through working, I'd like to talk to you some more about your case. We'll leave the door open so we can hear Abby if she needs you."

Her heart literally jumped. He wanted to be with her. And heaven help her, she wanted to be with him.

"Is there enough room on your sleeping bag for both of us to sprawl?"

His eyes gleamed mysteriously. "Let's find out."

It was crazy, unwise, but after lazing next to him at the park, she wasn't thinking straight and had no will to resist. In another minute he'd pulled the screen door across to keep the bugs from getting in. They lay down on their backs, side by side, to read and work.

The fragrance of honeysuckle was stronger than ever. Just knowing he was this close, there was no way she could concentrate on tonight's show. Helplessly she let the laptop slide off her and closed her eyes, never wanting to move from this spot.

Once in a while she stole a covert glance at Chaz. He was a remarkable, fantastic man whom she trusted implicitly. In another minute he put the reader aside and raised up on one elbow to look down at her. "Well done. You're an amazing writer, Lacey Pomeroy."

In a lightning move his dark head descended. When his mouth covered hers, it was no tentative kiss on his part. Unable to hold back, she opened her mouth to him. She'd been wanting this for days now. That moment on the swing had set her on fire. They came together in an explosion of need, something she'd been secretly dreaming about.

He rolled her toward him, thrusting one hand into her hair. His lips made a foray over her features, kissing every centimeter before claiming her mouth once more. Their legs got tangled. She wanted this to go on and on and never stop. To be alive again—he was making her feel immortal.

"Lacey?"

Through the mist of euphoria she heard her sister's voice.

Oh, no…

Embarrassed to be caught like this, she extricated herself from Chaz's arms. Hot faced, she got clumsily to her feet. Chaz stood up behind her. When she looked around, there was Ruth on the other side of the screen. Normally she didn't come to the condo until time for Lacey to leave for the radio station.

Her blue eyes could take on different shades, depending on her emotions. Right now they looked like cobalt as she took in the sight of them. Lacey had no idea how long she might have been standing there.

She was sorry her sister had seen them like this. Ruth might have a boyfriend at the moment, but Lacey knew her sister had been attracted to Chaz the second they'd been introduced.

"Abby's awake. She won't let me go into the bedroom. She wants Chaz."

He squeezed Lacey's arm. "I'll go to her," he whispered.

After picking up the reader and laptop, he stepped past her and opened the screen. "Thanks for the heads-up, Ruth. Abby had another scare today, with a wasp this time. I promised I'd inspect the window before she got up from her nap."

On his way through to the bedroom, he put the reader and laptop on the dining table. Lacey followed him. Her little redheaded cherub was waiting for him on the side of her bed, dangling her feet.

"Here I am, sweetheart. I'll check the window for you." She watched his every move. He raised the blinds. "No bees. See?"

She looked back at Lacey and ran to her. "It's in the toilet, Mommy."

"That's right. Say thank-you to Chaz."

"Thank you, Chaz." She darted to him. When he picked her up, she hugged him with all her might.

"You're welcome."

The three of them gravitated to the family room. Ruth was fixing herself something to eat. "There's no bees, Auntie Ruth."

But Lacey's sister wasn't listening. She was in one of her ugly moods, as their mom called them.

Chaz slipped past them and went out to the deck for his backpack. He glanced at Lacey as he came through again. "I need to get to the office. Good luck with tonight's program. See you later."

Just like that he'd vanished out the front door. After what had happened on the deck, Lacey felt a loss and knew she was in real trouble.

Ruth eyed her. "How come you were out there instead of your bedroom?"

"You know I would never go to bed with any man unless I were married to him. Having said that, I admit I'm very attracted to Chaz. I didn't know it was possible after Ted."

"It was so intense out there, the stalker could have snatched Abby and you wouldn't have known."

Lacey sucked in her breath. Her sister never minced words. She was used to that, but this time she'd gone too far. "That was cruel, Ruth. Especially when you know Chaz has men guarding the condo day and night."

"While he enjoys your phony engagement."

She'd never known Ruth to be this openly hostile

to her before. "He had his reasons for the engagement. They made sense to me and Mom."

Ruth ate one of Abby's apple slices. "Is he for real?"

"He's a real P.I. if that's what you mean. I've been to his office and met his boss."

"Have you stopped to consider he might pull this fiancé business on his other female clients? You know. To get a little on the side?"

Lacey frowned. "Where's all this coming from?"

"I watch a lot of *Law and Order.* Anyone can decide to be a P.I. and hang out a shingle. It doesn't mean he has any real experience. Seeing him making out with you on a summer afternoon instead of doing his job leads me to think you're being conned."

"Chaz was a navy SEAL for ten years before he became a P.I." Lacey hoped he would forgive her for telling Ruth, but her sister was behaving like an attack dog.

Ruth's eyebrows lifted. "I'll admit he's the personification of what most women imagine a SEAL would look like, but do you have proof?"

"His word," Lacey declared crisply.

Ruth shook her head. "Sometimes you're pathetically naive."

Lacey had taken enough. "I don't vet you about your boyfriends. The point is, I believe in Chaz, and until he gives me a reason not to trust him, I'll go along with his plan. He's been wonderful with Abby."

"If it gets him what he wants…" she said.

Ruth was enjoying baiting her. Lacey could feel it. Something was definitely wrong. "How did the job search go today?"

"What do you think? Every merchandising company

in Salt Lake uses big carriers and none of them are hiring right now."

That could be one explanation why Ruth was needling her mercilessly, but Lacey feared Ruth's jealousy over Chaz was at the bottom of this.

"Would you consider going back to your old job at the cell-phone company?"

"You didn't really ask me that question, did you?"

"I know it can't compare to being a pilot, but until things pick up, it would be better than nothing. Right?"

"Wrong. Let's put the shoe on the other foot. What if you couldn't get a radio show anywhere. Do you think you could sell phones for even one day without going berserk?"

Lacey wished she hadn't said anything. Wanting to smooth things over she said, "Do you have dinner plans?"

"No."

That emphatic answer didn't sound good coming from her sister. "I have an idea. Why don't I call Mom and the four of us can go for a pasta dinner. I'm sick of worrying about the stalker." She also needed something to get Chaz off her mind for a little while. "If we leave soon, I'll be back in plenty of time to get to the station for my program."

"Why not."

Chapter Eight

Chaz drove away from Lacey's home deep in thought. To his chagrin he didn't realize he was breaking the speed limit until a policeman pulled him over and gave him a ticket. He hadn't had one of those since he was a teen.

After he reached the office, he sat in his vehicle for a minute replaying the day's events. Ruth's return to the condo was unfortunate timing. He'd assumed she wouldn't be back from St. George until much later.

But on second thought, it was probably a good thing she'd shown up when she did. Hopefully what she'd seen, with Lacey locked in his embrace, would dampen any interest she might have in him.

As for Chaz, he was so on fire for Lacey, he could easily have lost his head out there on the deck. The chemistry between them had been building from the moment he'd looked into her eyes at the radio station. Since then, something magical had been happening to both of them. She couldn't have responded to him the way she did without desire driving her.

When he'd hugged Abby after being in her mother's arms, he knew it was imperative he catch her stalker before things went any further. He'd said that before, but now he really meant it.

"That's quite a conversation you're having with yourself."

Chaz jerked his head around to see his friend. "Mitch." He levered himself from the seat of the Forerunner.

"How's it going?"

Chaz pulled the speeding ticket out of his pocket and showed it to him.

Mitch chuckled. "I got one just like it in the same spot three weeks ago. They must be making a ton of money."

"That's what I thought," Chaz grumbled.

"Maybe I should have asked you how the engagement is going."

Chaz squinted at him. "For anyone else, that information is classified. But since it's you, I have to admit it's a double-edged sword."

"I believe it. Even so, is it producing results?"

Chaz rubbed the back of his neck. "Yes."

"Come into my office and let's talk."

They walked into the back room and headed down the hallway. Roman saw them and asked them to join him in his office for a minute.

"Mitch? Just wanted you to know I got the judge to issue that warrant for you to search the insurance office in the morning. You can pick it up at nine at the courthouse."

"Hallelujah."

Roman's dark eyes swerved to Chaz. "Chief Mahoney came through for you, too." Roman handed him a piece of paper with a name and number on it. "This woman is on the Albuquerque UFO committee. You call her after eight her time tonight and she'll try to answer your questions. If there's nothing else, I'm on my way home."

They thanked him before sequestering themselves in Mitch's office. Chaz sat down opposite the desk and stretched his legs. "Tell me something honestly," he said. "Have you ever gotten involved with a woman who was a client?"

"Not doing P.I. work, but there was a time in my marshal days when I got called in on a witness protection case. There was this woman who worked for the government. She knew classified information that could get her killed. I got too close to her. Luckily I didn't blow the operation, but I lost my concentration. Needless to say it never happened again."

"That's my problem. I can't promise that it won't happen again. I blew it today," Chaz confessed. He told Mitch what had happened without going into detail.

Mitch cocked his head. "Then don't go over there until you know she's home from the radio station and in bed. With her sister sleeping there, your problem's solved."

"You're right. I've got work to do and won't go near her until Thursday. I'm taking her and Abby to the soccer game."

Mitch's mouth curved in a half smile. "Travis told me. We're all anxious to meet this celebrity. We've decided we're going to listen to her show tonight."

"You'll be surprised how entertaining it is." Chaz got to his feet. "You going to be here long?"

"Afraid so. I'm backlogged with paperwork I need to clean up."

"Tell me about it. I'm going home and making the phone call that might tell me I'm getting close to her stalker."

"Good luck. Watch your back."

"Always."

Chaz left for home, intending to take his friend's advice. But he felt as if he'd just gone on a diet and was already experiencing deprivation. Worse, he'd finished Lacey's novel and was out of reading material. He could stop at a bookstore and pick up a new police procedural, but there'd be no thrill.

Lacey's story had enchanted him and he wanted more of the same. Since he couldn't be with her right now, maybe he'd download another YA sci-fi book. Although he doubted he'd enjoy it nearly as much.

When he got home, he fixed himself a couple of turkey sandwiches and downed them with a quart of milk. With a new pack of licorice in hand, he went into his study to make the call. He needed answers and hoped he was going to get them.

"Mrs. Bateman? This is Chaz Roylance. I'm investigating on a case and need some information."

"Oh, yes, I've been expecting your call. What can I do to help you?"

He tightened his grip on the phone. "Could you tell me how it would be possible for someone who's not on the UFO committee to be in possession of one of your official envelopes?"

"Well, I'm sure the printing company we use has some, but we keep the rest of them stored in boxes at my house. I have done so for the past five years."

Good. That's what he'd hoped for. "So when you

send out flyers, are you the one who stuffs them into the envelopes?"

"Elaine Stafford, who's on the committee, usually helps me."

"The next question I want to ask you may sound strange, but it's vital I get a correct answer from you."

"What is it?"

"What color is your hair?"

She chuckled. "That's strange, all right. I'm a brunette."

"Do you dye it?"

"No."

"So when you stuffed the envelopes for the coming seminar, you were a brunette."

"Yes."

"What about Elaine?"

"She has brownish hair."

"Her natural color, do you think?"

"Yes. She's only twenty-seven. I doubt she dyes it."

Chaz's pulse picked up speed. "Thank you. Now, excluding anyone from the printer's shop, could you explain how someone other than you or Elaine could get hold of an envelope for their own purposes?"

"Oh, I see what you're driving at. Of course. We have a mailing list we add to each year as people attend the seminar. Whenever there's a new event coming up, we send them a flyer and also enclose an envelope and flyer in the hope they'll spread the word. That's how we're building our program."

"So you have to fold the additional envelope and flyer to fit inside."

"Yes."

That's why the one sent to Lacey had looked creased.

"How long ago did you send a flyer announcing this weekend's seminar?"

"Five weeks ago. That gives everyone a chance to arrange flight schedules and hotel accommodations."

Five weeks. "Where did you go to mail them?"

"I always take the big committee mailings to the airport post office."

Chaz reached for another piece of licorice. "I'm sitting in front of my computer. Could you email me the complete list of people you sent flyers to for this weekend's seminar?"

"Yes. I'll do it right now, but I'll need to go into the other room to my computer."

"I'll wait. I may have more questions."

"Just a minute."

To his relief he didn't have to wait long. "I'm sending it now."

"I got it."

"This must be very important."

"It is. Believe me. Please stay on the line with me."

"Of course."

Two hundred and twenty-four names were on the list. Amazing to see that many people would attend a UFO conference. He zeroed in on the familiar ones from Lacey's list of people. Her name was there, naturally.

Then he went through the whole list alphabetically. He came to the *G*s and was surprised when he saw Ruth's name. Chaz hadn't known she went to those seminars. Lacey'd never mentioned that her sister was also interested in UFOs. He would have to ask her about that.

"Mrs. Bateman? There's a name here I'm curious

about. Ruth Garvey. Can you tell me when she first started showing up on your mailing list?"

"I'll check the lists for the past five years. It's all I have."

Again he had to wait. In a few minutes she came back on. "She's on last year's list only."

Adrenaline shot through him. That meant she'd attended last year's seminar, or at least registered for it. He would verify that information with Lacey. "What was her mailing address?"

"Idaho Falls, Idaho."

"I need her street address and telephone number."

The woman complied.

"Thank you, Mrs. Bateman. You've been more helpful than you could possibly know."

"Since it's official police business, I was glad to do it. Goodbye."

The second he hung up Chaz called Lon. "I still need you to follow Ruth Garvey in the morning. If she leaves her car at the airport again, wait for Jim to show up. He'll relieve you so he can watch her car until she gets back to the airport. I also need something else from you."

"Shoot."

"There's a phone number I'd like you to check out in the morning. When you learn anything, call me. If I don't answer, just leave a message on my voice mail." Chaz gave him the information and the reason for it.

"I'll get on it first thing."

"I can always count on you. Thanks, Lon. Keep me posted."

Thoughts bombarded Chaz's mind, chilling him so badly he didn't want to put them into words. Not yet...

Tomorrow he had a plane to catch to Idaho Falls. He drew out his wallet and removed all his ID. In its place he supplied fake credentials for himself, then made a round-trip reservation online for early in the morning.

With that matter taken care of, he had a long night to face. The next best thing to being with Lacey was listening to her.

He turned on the radio. Her program had already started. Chaz sat through the next three hours thinking hard about her case, making more notes, checking and rechecking facts. When she went off the air, he headed for her condo, hoping to heaven that what he was thinking wasn't true. He planned to fly to Idaho in the morning to help *prove* that it wasn't true.

From the start, his instincts had told him Lacey was being menaced by a woman. The patterns pointed to it for many reasons. But it had never occurred to him it might be her own flesh and blood. One, furthermore, who had total access to Abby.

When he'd left the SEALs, he'd promised himself and the Almighty that he would never deal with a female enemy again.

Once more, the past's debilitating, haunting blackness began to seep through him, robbing him of the joy of listening to the woman whose kiss had shaken him to the core today.

LACEY HAD LISTENED ALL Wednesday morning in case Chaz phoned to check in with her. She was a complete wreck, having tossed and turned through the night, angry with herself for going out on the deck with him in the first place. He'd seen through her as though she were a plate-glass window. She'd left herself wide-open and had made a perfect fool of herself.

Not even with Ted had she behaved that way before—not in the beginning, anyway. The excuse that she was being stalked didn't wash. She'd loved it that Chaz had bought her book and was enjoying it. Somehow she'd felt closer to him because of it and he knew it. Her attraction to him had stood out a mile.

Ruth had been right about a lot of things. Lacey would never have agreed to a mock engagement if she hadn't already been spellbound by Chaz's compelling aura. Her sister had voiced the possibility that Chaz was in the habit of getting close to his female clients. Ruth was probably right. How embarrassing was it that when he'd first questioned her, she'd told him no man had interested her since Ted. She couldn't imagine being with another man.

What a joke!

By now he likely believed she wasn't the innocent she purported to be and had been lying about being unaware of Ken's interest, too.

She couldn't take back those minutes when she'd kissed Chaz with a hunger that had shocked her. To think Ruth had witnessed their embrace made it all the more humiliating. The only thing Lacey could do was never let it happen again.

Miserable and at loose ends, she called her mom, who told her to bring Abby over. They'd all have lunch and spend the rest of the day together. Abby loved seeing her nana. It was a good thing, since Lacey was going crazy with her own thoughts. To sit around waiting for Chaz to call was childish and ridiculous. He was a P.I., for heaven's sake, doing his best to help capture this monster.

On her way to the car, she stopped at the mailbox and put the small pile of delivered mail in her bag. Chaz had told her not to open it until he was with her. If he was there when she got home from the radio station tonight, she'd leave it on the table for him to do the honors and hurry to bed.

She didn't think she could handle finding another death threat. There was something so hideous about the thought of a person actually composing words to terrorize her.

So far no one seemed to have been following her, let alone attempting to attack her. Chaz's presence had no doubt prevented her stalker from doing anything more than making harassing phone calls and sending threats. But Chaz couldn't go on doing this forever.

Lacey believed in Chaz, but the longer this went on, the harder it would be to hide the way she felt about him. She'd been in his arms and tasted his mouth. No way could she forget what that had been like.

NOTHING IN THIS BUSINESS worked without precision timing and cooperation. After Chaz returned from Idaho Falls, he checked with Adam, who told him Lacey had just left the condo with her daughter. As for Jim, he was still at the airport watching Ruth's car.

Hearing that news, Chaz phoned Roman, who arranged for Simon Evans, the same forensics expert who'd discovered the hair samples in the envelope, to meet him at Lacey's place ASAP.

"Thanks for getting here so fast. We only have a short window of time in case Mrs. Pomeroy decides to return." He walked the other man through to the guest bedroom where Ruth slept. He hoped the sheets and pillowcase she'd slept on hadn't been washed yet.

"If you'll check this room and the guest bathroom across the hall for samples of DNA, those are the only areas I need covered."

It didn't take Simon long to do his business. Chaz walked him out to his car. "I appreciate you doing this."

"Happy to oblige, but I probably won't have results before Monday. You have no idea of my backlog."

"No problem. I'm indebted to you."

Once the man drove off, Chaz left for his own home. By Monday he and Lacey would be back from Albuquerque. If Simon's work produced a match to the hair in the envelope, then the case was solved and Ruth was the stalker. And then another nightmare would begin for Lacey and her family. The pain they'd go through knowing it was their daughter and sister would be horrendous.

He could be wrong about Ruth, though he didn't think so. His trip to Idaho had provided more of the kind of information he'd been looking for.

After arranging for a rental car that morning, he'd driven to the few air cargo companies listed. None of his questions produced results. His last stop was at Landis Air Cargo. He approached the fortyish-looking guy at the counter.

"Hi. I'm Don Archer and I've just moved here from Portland. A while back I happened to meet a pilot of your company and she told me you could do a good job for me handling my computer-merchandise business."

"That's nice to hear. Who was it?"

"I only remember her first name. Ruth something."

The other man shook his head. "No one by that name has ever worked here. One of our pilots, Bruce Larson, lives with a woman named Ruth."

"Is she a brunette?"

"No. Blonde."

"Then she's not the one. I've come to the wrong place, but it doesn't matter. As long as I'm here, do you provide service to Albuquerque? That's one of my new markets."

He nodded. "It's one of our oldest routes. Take a look on the wall chart. We fly a lot of places."

Chaz gave it a quick glance. Their reach included Colorado, Wyoming, Nevada, Utah, Oregon and of course Idaho. Except for Oregon, those were the places where the phone calls and death threats had originated.

He could hear Lacey's question. *How can this stalker be in so many places almost at the same time?*

"That's all I wanted to know. Thanks. I'll be back."

Leaving the air cargo company, Chaz drove his rental car to the address Mrs. Bateman had given him. It was an apartment in an eightplex. No one answered the door. He checked the mailboxes. B. Larson was one of the tenants. In case Larson was an accomplice to the stalking, Chaz didn't ask questions of any of the tenants coming and going from the building—it might get back to Mr. Larson.

New information revealed Ruth hadn't worked as a pilot in Idaho Falls. Besides living with a pilot, what had she been doing? Why had she come home to Salt Lake this past month? Her family knew nothing about her or her activities. Chaz's mind flooded with more questions demanding answers.

He got back into the rental car and phoned Lon,

whose input revealed that there was no phone listing for Ruth in Idaho. The number Mrs. Bateman had given him off the application Ruth had filled out for the UFO convention belonged to someone else. The phone company claimed it had never been assigned to Ruth Garvey. Not only that, it didn't match the cell-phone number Mrs. Garvey had given Chaz for Ruth when they'd met the first time.

Armed with the knowledge that it *could* have been Ruth, with the help of her boyfriend, who'd sent Lacey that envelope from Albuquerque last Friday, he'd flown home, anxious to get the DNA samples gathered from Ruth's bedroom while Lacey's condo was empty.

He drove back to his office and looked at the photograph Lacey had given him of her core group. Three of the women and two of the men had various kinds of blond hair. One of the men wore his to the shoulders. It could have shed a seven-inch-long strand. But it was difficult to tell the actual color from a picture. He had yet to meet Jennifer, who was also a blonde.

Chaz pulled a cola from the office fridge and took a gulp. If Ruth's DNA didn't match the hair samples in the envelope, then he was back at square one. After he went to Albuquerque, his list might grow depending on the number of blonds on the UFO committee. In that case Roman would have to arrange for interstate cooperation to get a judge to order samples of DNA taken from each of them.

As he finished off his drink and tossed it into the wastebasket, the thought came to him that maybe it was Bruce Larson's hair that had gotten into the envelope.

Neither Lacey nor her mother had ever met Bruce, so no one knew what he looked like. But *Lon* knew. He said he'd seen Ruth talking to a guy before the plane took off at the small airport.

Chaz got him on his cell phone. "A question for you, Lon."

"Shoot."

"This guy who's been flying Ruth around. What color hair does he have?"

"He's a blond. Shaggy."

"Thanks for the info."

Chaz headed for Lacey's condo thinking about several new possibilities. If Ruth had gotten Bruce involved, then they could be coconspirators. More than ever, he needed to know the results of that DNA report. If one of the hairs was Ruth's, then Chaz needed a DNA sample from Bruce Larson. He would call Roman and see what could be arranged to get a sample from the pilot while Chaz flew to Albuquerque with Lacey.

To ease his fears, he phoned Lacey and told her Tom would be staying inside the condo with Ruth and Abby until the radio program was over. "It's a precaution I feel is necessary now that we're getting so close to exposing the culprit." She didn't fight him.

Chapter Nine

Lacey stayed at her mother's until time to go home and put Abby down for the night. Her daughter talked about Chaz quite incessantly. It was only natural. She'd been only two when Ted was killed, and there'd been no other men in their lives until Chaz. He'd brought gifts and rescued her from a wasp. He'd played ball with her at the park and put her on the swing with him. What more could a little girl want from the most exciting man in existence?

Tom, one of Chaz's crew, arrived while Lacey was getting ready for her radio program. He said he would work at the kitchen table. Then Ruth let herself in with more bad news about the job situation. But after being introduced to Tom, who wasn't bad looking, she didn't seem to mind that she had company.

Lacey peeked in on Abby one more time before leaving for her car. Her heart leaped when she saw Chaz's Forerunner pull into the guest space. When he got out, she noticed he was wearing a tan jacket over an open-necked shirt and khakis. The sight of him made her stomach flip.

He smiled at her through veiled eyes. "Perfect timing,

I'd say. Is Tom upstairs?" She nodded. "Good. Come get into my car. I'll drive you to the radio station."

Chaz walked to the passenger door of his car and opened it. She climbed inside. "I got here as soon as I could. I need to ask you a few questions. No better time than now. Once your broadcast is over, we'll both be too tired to concentrate on your case."

But hopefully not too tired to concentrate on each other.

She wasn't sure what to think, but she was aware this was a different Chaz than she'd seen before. He'd been the total professional when she'd first met him, but tonight he was...masterful. There was no other way to describe him. Something had changed.

Maybe he was letting her know that what had happened on the deck was an accident and there'd be no repeats. Then again his demeanor could have more to do with the investigation.

"So you honestly believe you're getting closer to finding the stalker?" As they drove off, she gave him a sideward glance. What she saw sent a shiver through her body. In the semidark, his black brows and hardened jaw gave him a slightly forbidding cast.

"I *know* I am," his voice grated. The authority in his tone left her in no doubt he was speaking the truth.

"Can you tell me anything?" she asked softly.

"Not yet. I'm curious about something. Have I got this straight that the summer solstice seminar in Milwaukee and the UFO seminar in Albuquerque are held a week apart?"

"Yes, but that's not unusual. There are dozens of paranormal conventions going on all over the country at any given time. Those two just happen to be close together. Normally I would never schedule them back-to-back, but they're two of the most important ones for me."

"Has your mother ever gone to any of these seminars with you?"

"Only one in Salt Lake this year, just to see what goes on. It didn't make her want to become a regular."

Lacey thought he might smile. Instead he said, "What about Ruth?"

"She went to the one in Albuquerque a year ago to help me out. It was right after the funeral. I was supposed to be on the program. She read the speech I'd prepared weeks earlier. Unfortunately she had to take time off work. I paid for her flight down and back. Why do you ask?"

"Only that Ruth could provide some eyes and ears. She was there and undoubtedly met the people on the committee. Maybe she saw something she didn't know was important. I'll ask her later."

They pulled into the back of the radio station and he shut off the engine. "One last question. Why did Ruth tell me about Shelley instead of you?"

Lacey blinked in surprise. "Are you talking about Shelley Marlow?"

"If that's her last name."

"She was Ted's girlfriend before he met me."

"Your sister seems to think she might be someone to add to the list."

"That was a long time ago. I'd forgotten about her."

"How long did he date her?"

"A month. She had a hard time getting over Ted."

"How hard?" he persisted.

Chaz and her sister had covered a lot of ground in

the short time they'd spoken. But then he was a P.I. in the middle of a stalking case, gathering information as fast as he could. With his rare brand of heady male charisma, Ruth was more than a little interested in him.

"She called him a lot before we were married."

"In other words, she was intrusive."

"Yes. She'd stay on the phone and sob."

"After only knowing him a month?"

Lacey nodded. "Ted said he'd already decided to stop seeing her before he met me."

"How did they meet?"

"She was a college student from Long Beach. They met at a party at Rob Sharp's house. He was in the Coast Guard, too, and best man at our wedding. I put him on the list I made up for you."

"I remember," Chaz murmured. "Did Shelley come to your wedding?"

"No. Ted wouldn't have invited her. After our honeymoon she started up the calling again. He warned her to leave him alone, so she wrote to him instead. He didn't answer her letters. She wrote three, then they stopped. I haven't thought about her since."

Chaz's black brows furrowed. "Ruth said she came to the funeral."

Incredulous, Lacey stared at him. "That's impossible. For one thing, Ruth wouldn't have known who she was. Neither would I. I never saw a picture of her. If Ruth found out somehow that Shelley was there, why didn't she tell me?"

"Is it possible she could have forgotten at the time?"

"Maybe."

"We'll talk to her about it later." He pulled the keys

out of the ignition. "Sorry for putting you through the interrogation, but it's part of the process."

"I realize that."

His compelling mouth broke into the first smile tonight. "I'll have you know I'm looking forward to taking you and Abby to the soccer game tomorrow. A whole crowd from my work will be there with their families. Sydney has a little four-year-old girl named Cindy, her second child. She and Abby will probably get along famously."

Lacey took a deep breath. "A ball game sounds like exactly what I need to get my mind off everything."

"That makes two of us. Don't be concerned if the guys play it up about our pseudo engagement. They're hard-core teases."

She laughed, but inside she moaned because she didn't want to think about the day she would have to give the ring back. She was getting used to wearing it. Lately she'd been wishing that what she had with Chaz was real.

His gaze studied her mouth, fanning the flame burning inside her. "You need to laugh more often."

Averting her eyes, she reached for the door handle and got out. "I need to hurry inside or my broadcast will start without me."

"I have a phone call to make, then I'm going to listen to your program in the surveillance van parked over there while Adam and I look at tapes. If you want to give my friends a thrill, say hi to Travis and Mitch while you're on the air. They'll be listening tonight."

"You're serious?" The thought of it tickled her.

"You'll find out tomorrow at the soccer game. See you after you're through with your show. When we get back to the condo, let's watch your DVD of *Otherworld*."

Her limbs felt as if they'd just turned to mush. "It's a fun old TV show, but you'll probably think it's corny."

"That's exactly the kind of thing I feel like watching tonight."

Me, too. With you. Alone.

She hurried away.

WHEN THE BLAZE OF RED GOLD disappeared inside the building, Chaz accessed the file on his computer from his iPhone and called Rob Sharp's number. It was only quarter to eight in California, not too late to be phoning him if he was around.

His wife answered. When he identified himself as a friend of Lacey Pomeroy's and asked if he could speak to her husband, she told him to hold on. In a minute he came to the phone.

"Hi! This is Rob. You say you're Lacey's friend?"

"Yes." After telling him he was a P.I. and explaining he was trying to catch Lacey's stalker, the other guy sobered. "If I thought you were her stalker, I wouldn't be having this conversation with you. You have brown hair. I've already identified the stalker as a blond."

After a long pause Rob said, "She's really being stalked?"

"She and Abby. I need some vital information and hope you can supply it."

"I'll tell you whatever I can. Lacey's the best."

"I agree. Do you remember Shelley Marlow, the girl Ted was dating before he met Lacey?"

"Sure. She went to my high school."

"What was she like?"

"She was a nice girl, but I should never have lined them up because I didn't know she was so fragile. He took her out a few times and realized it was a mistake. Unfortunately she didn't understand the word *no* and refused to give up on him. He finally had to put her straight."

"That's what Lacey said. Tell me something. I know you were at Ted's funeral. Did you see her there?"

"She couldn't have been there."

"Why? Someone else said they saw her."

"That would have been impossible. Shelley died about two years ago. In the paper it said natural causes, but I think she was on drugs and overdosed."

The air froze in Chaz's lungs. Either Ruth had made an honest mistake, or she'd told another lie. This one couldn't be swept under the rug.

"That's all I needed to hear. You've been more helpful than you know. Do me a favor and don't tell Lacey I called. When I've caught her stalker, I'll tell her to phone you herself with the good news."

Chaz clicked off and joined Adam in the van. To his surprise, the other guy already had Lacey's show on. Listening to it wasn't one of his duties. The announcer was just giving the intro. "And now here's the founder and host of the Stargrazer program, Lacey Pomeroy."

"Hello, everyone out there. It's a beautiful evening and there's no other place I'd rather be than right here, anxious to talk to all you callers. Stewart tells me the phone calls are lined up. I promise to keep things moving, but before I get started, I'd like to welcome two new listeners who've just discovered the show.

"Mitch and Travis, if you've got your radios on, welcome to my paranormal world. I can promise you thrills and chills." Chaz grinned. The guys would love this. "If you decide to call in, I'm sure Stewart will fit you into the lineup. And now let's take our first caller. It's Glen from Fayetteville, Arkansas."

Chaz glanced at Adam. "I didn't know you liked her program."

He smiled. "I've been enjoying it since you put me on the case. How would you like to introduce me to her after you've caught the creep harassing her?"

Gritting his teeth, Chaz said, "I'll ask her if she's agreeable."

"I'll owe you big-time. She's a knockout and has more going on upstairs than any woman I've ever known. Did you hear her the other night poking holes through some guy's theory because his physics were all wrong? She mops the floor with any pseudointellectual who tries to take her on. I like a woman with her kind of brains, you know?"

"As a matter of fact, I *do* know. If you really want to get inside the creative part of her head, read her young-adult fantasy. I've got a copy of it you can borrow, but it's at the condo. I'll give it to you tomorrow."

"Thanks. She's sure got a cute little girl. Looks just like her. Her curls bob when she does that circle thing." It was her butterfly walk, but Chaz kept that to himself. "Can you believe hair grows that color? It's so beautiful it's unreal."

Chaz liked Adam a lot, but he'd heard about as much of this kind of chat as he could handle. He'd played with that hair, kissed it while he was devouring her ardent mouth. She'd been hungry for him, too. If it hadn't been for Ruth… He sucked in his breath. "I agree."

"Her sister's nice looking, too. Runs in the family obviously, but I have my eye on Mrs. Pomeroy."

"Understood." Once you'd seen her, she ruined you for other women. "Let's see what you got on tape today." While Chaz listened, he turned on the screen.

Various people were leaving the condo building to go to work. Soon Ruth appeared in designer jeans and a tank top. She talked on her cell phone all the way to her Mazda and was still talking as she drove off.

He fast-forwarded the tape and suddenly there was Lacey in white denims and a summery plaid blouse walking out to her car with Abby. She stopped at the mailbox and put whatever was in there in her purse. He noticed with satisfaction that Abby, dressed in a pink top and shorts, was hugging the big nesting doll under her arm.

If he were alone, he would have played the tape of her again. Once he'd seen everything on it, he turned off the screen and found a seat to listen to the last of the broadcast. The calls just kept coming.

"Stewart tells me he's got Travis on the line."

Hearing her mention his friend's name, Chaz sat forward. Adam rolled his eyes at him. "Is that *our* Travis?"

"The one and only."

"So, Travis, where do you hail from?"

"West Texas."

"I guess I don't have to tell you that up in those Davis Mountains is one of the best places in the U.S. to look at the stars. Folks? It's so dark up there, with your naked eye you can see falling stars zipping through space."

"Yup. I've spent many a night out there watching for them."

"You're one of *us,* Travis, you just didn't know it until now. I have an astronomer friend who runs the observatory up there."

"You know about that?"

She'd surprised Travis. Chaz was loving this.

"I spent a semester there while I was in school."

"Doing what?

"Geophysics. We were studying one of Jupiter's moons, looking for water." Even Chaz hadn't known of the exact project she'd been working on. "While there I got the idea for a new sci-fi novel, but that's another story for another day. Thanks for calling in. Don't be a stranger, now, y'all hear?" she teased with a fetching, authentic-sounding Texas drawl.

Lacey...

"The next person on the line is Scott from Fairbanks, Alaska. He told my producer something strange is going on up there. Lights are everywhere in the sky, but they're not the aurora borealis because it isn't visible this time of year. Tell us what's happening, Scott. We want to know exactly what you're seeing."

"You're a freakin' bitch who'd believe anything." The sound of the male-enhanced voice drove Chaz to his feet. He recognized the distortion technology being employed by the caller. *"Well, believe this, bit—"*

Stewart must have pressed the cut-off button, but Lacey would have heard enough to be traumatized.

"Too bad there's an occasional caller who uses this show to vent his frustrations," she spoke again, her delivery calm and seamless. She was incredible. "But America's a free country. That's what makes it the greatest place to live on Earth, right? Our next caller is Shay from New Orleans."

Chaz couldn't get out of the van and into the station fast enough. The look of relief when Lacey saw him enter Stewart's booth told him he'd done the right thing. For the rest of the show she would eye him from time to time, needing that support. He wanted her to need him. He wanted her to need him so badly she wouldn't want to lose him when this was all over.

After her show ended, he ushered her through the radio station to the door. The night watchman had heard about their engagement and congratulated them before Chaz helped her into his Forerunner.

"You were magnificent, Lacey." He hugged her to him for a moment before letting her go. He couldn't help himself. "When the call came in, Adam and I were listening to your show in the van. As soon as I reached Stewart's booth, I tried to locate the caller, but it must have come from one of those prepaid cellular phones, because I couldn't trace it."

She eyed him earnestly. "It's because of you that it didn't bother me that much. I hate it that someone's out there determined to kill me, but the shock value is beginning to wear off."

"You're beating this person at their own sick game. I can't tell you how proud I am of the way you handled it. Stewart's in awe of you."

"Good old Stewart. He cut off that stalker so fast, the maniac probably didn't know what hit him."

Chaz chuckled. "I don't think Travis knew what hit him, either. You're an exciting woman. Even Adam, one of my support crew, is captivated by your show." *And you.* "You can add another couple of fans to your millions."

"Hardly millions, but a comment like that makes Barry's day."

How different she was from Ruth. The one craved attention, the other eschewed it. So went the history of siblings.

They drove back to Lacey's condo. The second Tom saw them at the door, he nodded to Chaz and went out to the van.

When they walked in, Ruth was still up, talking on her iPhone in the living room. Lacey asked him if he wanted a soda. He nodded and followed her into the kitchen. Ruth soon caught up to them.

Lacey turned to her. "How did things go?"

"Quiet on both counts." Lacey took that to mean Ruth kept to herself.

"I know. She's so good. Do you want a soda, too?"

"No, thanks. I'm going to bed."

"Before you do, I wanted to ask you something."

"Shoot."

"Chaz said you told him Shelley Marlow came to the funeral."

"Yeah. She introduced herself."

"Why didn't you say anything to me at the time?"

"I told Mom while we were in the hearse, but she decided you didn't need to know. You were grieving so much over Ted, she didn't want to burden you during the funeral. I agreed with her. But now that you're being stalked, I thought Chaz should know. She was sick."

Lacey nodded. "Maybe she has been the one all along. I got another threat tonight during my broadcast."

Ruth flicked Chaz a glance. "Any luck tracing it?"

"None, but I'm not worried. I have other leads and

it won't be much longer now. Do you want to stay up and watch *Otherworld* with us?"

"Sorry, but all that sci-fi crap really is the dregs."

Ruth's vitriol was spilling out, but she didn't care. Had Lacey always had to put up with the nasty side of her sister, or was this behavior worse than usual? "After tonight's program, I'm in the mood for more of it."

"I'll make popcorn," Lacey piped up.

"Good night." Ruth wheeled away.

Within a few minutes all was quiet. Lacey made good on her offer. Soon she sat next to Chaz on the couch in the family room while they watched the first episode and ate popcorn. Since the death of his wife, this was the kind of night he'd forgotten existed.

"In case you get hooked, I thought you'd better see the beginning. It starts in Egypt at the Great Pyramid. The reason I like the show so much is that they're a really cute and resourceful family who adapt fast after they're transported to this different world. I would've loved to have been a writer for this show. Now I promise I'll stop talking."

Low laughter rolled out of Chaz. When there was no more popcorn, he put his arm around Lacey. She rested her head against him and they settled down to watch the show. Corny or not, he liked it.

Lacey was right. A good cast had been chosen to portray the family of four. It was the kind of family he'd pictured having one day. With Lacey's warm curvy body nestled against him, he could imagine she was his wife, and he was feeling better than good. Her subtle fragrance teased his senses. She would have been beautiful while she carried Abby.

How would it be to make her pregnant, knowing the little boy or girl inside was part of him and her?

"Do you want to see the second episode?" Lacey had asked the question, but he was slow on the uptake, not having realized the first one had ended.

"I'm crazy about the idea."

"Sure you are." She half laughed.

"I like the show, but sitting next to you any longer isn't a good idea. It makes me want to take up where we left off out on the deck." He planted a thorough kiss on her mouth. For a few minutes they forgot everything else and gave in to their passion. But things were heating up so fast that they'd need to move to the bedroom. To his chagrin, they weren't alone in the condo.

He found the strength to tear his lips from hers. "Much as I'd love to go on kissing you till morning, until I've caught your stalker, I promised myself to try to keep my wits about me. Otherwise you're going to think I had ulterior motives for becoming your temporary fiancé."

Lacey shut off the TV and DVD player with the remote and got up from the couch. "I promised myself the same thing," she said and hurried into the kitchen with the empty bowl. That kiss had gotten away from both of them.

He eyed her from a distance. "I'm going to brush my teeth, so I'll say good-night now. Thanks for a perfect ending to the day. Be ready at four tomorrow. I'll come by for you and Abby. We'll eat dinner out before the soccer game. "

"That's sounds exciting. Good night."

When Chaz bedded down for the night outside, he thought he might not fall asleep for a while, but to his surprise he must have passed out. The next thing he knew, he heard someone knocking. Opening his eyes, he saw Abby on the other side of the glass door. She was still in her jammies.

He sat up and slid it open. It was twenty to seven in the morning. He'd slept later than usual. "Well, hi, sweetheart. Are you awake?"

"Yes."

She was crying softly. "What's wrong?"

"My teeny baby's gone."

"Did you look inside your big-girl bag?" That was what Lacey called the bag she was holding on to.

"Yes. It's not here."

"Do you want me to look again?"

"Yes." She came closer and plopped it next to him.

He opened the bag and took the items out one by one. The nesting dolls weren't in there because he knew she kept them on her windowsill. She had a conglomeration of treasures, even a GoPhone. It was a cheap kind of cellular phone. When prepaid with cash, the call couldn't be traced. It looked new. "Is this your mommy's?"

"No."

"Then who does it belong to?"

"I don't know. I found it."

"Where?"

"In Auntie Ruth's closet."

"I see."

He'd seen Ruth talking on the phone last night, but she'd used an iPhone like Lacey's. Chaz closed his eyes tightly for a moment. Everything confirmed what he suspected. Then he turned the bag upside down and shook it.

"Your teeny baby isn't in here, but we'll find it. I bet you left it at your nana's house, or it's in your mommy's car. Go into your mommy's room and tell her I need her car keys to find it."

"Okay. Don't go away."

"I won't."

The second she ran off, he pulled out his iPhone and took a picture to prove that the GoPhone was in with the toys. Then he put everything back except the phones. After getting dressed, he slipped both phones into his backpack.

As he was locking the deck door behind him, a tousle-headed, red-haired Lacey appeared barefoot in the kitchen wearing jeans and a pink T-shirt. Some people didn't look good when they'd just been awakened from sleep. With that combination of her red hair and pink T-shirt, she'd never looked more delectable.

Her blue eyes were still foggy with sleep. "Good morning. What happened?" She smoothed some curls away from her cheek.

"Abby came out to the deck crying because she couldn't find her teeny nesting doll in the toy bag." He handed the bag to Lacey. "We went through it, but it wasn't there. I told her I'd go out to your car and search for it."

"Oh, honey, it's here on the counter next to the toaster." Lacey retrieved the doll and handed it to her. Abby made a crooning sound and walked around with it and her blanket pressed against her cheek.

He smiled. "Crisis averted."

"Yes," she said with a half laugh. "I'm sorry she wakened you."

"Since I've never had a child, I loved it that she came to me for help."

"You're her hero."

He felt the warmth of her gaze clear through him.

"I couldn't handle seeing her in tears."

"I know what you mean. Since you're still here and we're all up, would you like to stay and eat breakfast with us?"

"I wish I could, but I've got a full day ahead of me." While she followed him with her eyes, he picked up the reader from the dining room table and put it in his pack. "I'm taking this to the office. Adam wants to read your novel."

"You're kidding!"

"No. After doing surveillance, he's developed quite a crush on you."

It was fun watching color come through her fabulous skin. "I'll see you at four," he said, heading for the front door.

Abby chased after him and caught his leg. "Don't go."

It astonished him how powerfully she tugged on his heart. He hunkered down. "I have to go to work, but I'll see you later. We're going to go to a soccer game."

"What's soccer?"

He flicked Lacey a glance. "Your mommy will explain."

"Okay. Bye, Chaz." She threw her arms around his neck and gave him a kiss on the cheek. His first from her. He thought of it as his angel peck.

Once outside, he saw there was no sign of Ruth's red Mazda in the parking area. She always left early and this morning was no exception. Abby must have heard her on her way out and woken up.

After he got into his car, he reached into the backpack for the GoPhone and undid the back of it. The SIM card was missing, but the International Mobile Equipment Identity number was there on the inside plate. He'd take the phone to Roman and show him the picture evidence he'd shot with his iPhone. If a forensics expert from the police department had been with him, the other man would have taken a picture. As it was, he followed procedure. Roman could arrange for a subpoena to trace it to the account holder.

Since seeing the phone, he felt as if he'd been punched in the gut. In Abby's innocence, she'd provided a piece of evidence that might prove her aunt's guilt. Chaz was saying *might* right now because so far, there could be a plausible explanation for Ruth's behavior that had nothing to do with the case.

Ruth was a liar, but it didn't necessarily follow she was the stalker. Still…

En route to the office he phoned Mitch. "Forgive me for calling you this early, but I've got to talk or I'm not going to make it." Roman wouldn't be at the office yet.

"I've never heard you sound like this before. Hold on and let me grab the coffee I was making. Then I'm all yours."

The seconds passed like hours.

"I'm back. Now, tell me what's wrong."

"You might as well ask what *isn't* wrong."

"Lacey doesn't feel the same way you do? I don't believe it."

"No. I'd stake my life on the fact that her attraction to me is just as powerful. It's getting harder to keep my distance. That's the problem. I'm going down a path I don't think I can handle any longer."

"What do you mean?"

"Ever since I met her, I intended that when the case was over, I'd explore what's going on between us. But the closer I'm getting to the truth, the more terrified I am that I'm going to lose Lacey."

"You're not making sense. Once you find the person who's harassing her, I don't see you having a problem."

"It's not that simple, Mitch. When I tell you what happened to me near the end of my time in the SEALs, you'll better understand why this is tearing my guts out."

For the next little while Chaz unloaded on him. It was the first time he'd told anyone about the most horrific period of his life. "After I got out, I promised myself I'd never put myself in that position again. It's why I didn't go into law enforcement. Roman's firm offered me challenges where I could use my skills in ways that wouldn't put me in any more untenable positions. Or so I thought.

"When the call from Barry Winslow came in to the office, I asked Roman if I could be the one to take on this stalker. Wouldn't you know I made the classic mistake of assuming it was a man? I wanted to protect Lacey and her daughter. After what I'd come up against in the SEALs, I saw this as my opportunity to *help* a woman. Maybe then the nightmares would go away."

"I hear you, Chaz. That makes a lot of sense."

"I thought it did, too, until I started building this case. The signs began pointing to a woman. You know—no physical attacks made, phone calls and emails as the form of harassment. But by then I was already in too deep. My feelings for Lacey are so strong, I've never known anything like them and haven't been able to walk away. But it's what I should have done." He groaned. "Now that things are coming together, I'm terrified of where it's leading."

"You're talking about one of her best friends. That's tough, all right," he murmured in compassion.

"Except that since I had breakfast with you and Travis, they're no longer at the top of my list of suspects," he corrected Mitch. "There've been new revelations." Without preamble Chaz brought him up to speed on the conversation he'd had with Ruth and all the lies she'd told.

"You're telling me the stalker is Lacey's *sister?*"

"I'm ninety-nine percent positive. Lacey said her sister changed after their father died." One thing Chaz had learned about the father/daughter relationship: it was usually the first long-term male/female relationship for a woman. To lose him at a crucial age could be devastating.

"She's a loose cannon, Mitch. I mean, for all I know she wears a concealed weapon. If she thought I was onto her and drew a gun on me... I simply can't take that chance. I feel like I'm back in South America confronting a situation that's eating me alive. That's why I got out before. Now here I am again, but this time it's double jeopardy."

"What do you mean?"

Chaz had reached the office and pulled into his parking spot. "You think Lacey will ever look at me the same way again when she learns I suspect her sister? That I've suspected Ruth for the last few days and haven't told her? Lacey deserves the right to know I think her sister's the stalker. But I could be wrong. Until I get the results of the DNA, that's the hell of it."

"You're never wrong. By getting her to go along with the pretend engagement, look what's happened! You've solved her case with lightning speed. Moving in with her changed the whole dynamic for her sister. Ruth wasn't careful and that phone Abby found is a dead giveaway."

"I agree, but—"

"But you're worried that when you tell Lacey, she'll shoot the messenger."

"Yes," he muttered. "I couldn't bear it if she accused me of jeopardizing her life and Abby's because I didn't yet have the DNA proof. I have to tell her what I know. But maybe I should let someone else handle the case from now on."

"Why? Tell Lacey the truth today when you're not around her sister. Whatever follows will be dealt with by the arresting officer when Ruth is apprehended. In that regard you will have been honest with Lacey, and you'll still be keeping the promise you made to yourself when you got out of the SEALs. The police will take care of the suspect. You won't have to do battle with a woman."

What Mitch said made sense, but Chaz was afraid Lacey would turn on him when he told her his suspicions about Ruth. His prime suspect was her sister! How would anyone handle news like that? He'd be walking on shaky ground with her, but he knew in his gut he had no other choice.

He took a long, deep breath. "I owe you big-time for listening to me, Mitch."

"Then we're even because I've unloaded on you

more times than I dare admit. Hang in there. It sounds like it's almost over. You know we're in your corner all the way."

"I know. Thanks." He clicked off.

Roman had just driven in. Chaz got out of the car to approach him.

Chapter Ten

"In the midfield I see another familiar face. Will Johnson makes his anticipated return in the middle of a firestorm. His shot was blocked by Rimando. A good ball to Noyes. And the foul by Gonzalez. We may have a charge coming. It's a bad foul, but he got away with it before. Yes, it's a foul. A red card is coming. Yes. Gonzalez is gone and done!

"There goes the sign for three minutes. Ten men apiece now. Jory is looking for Findley. Cooper just laid a beautiful ball at his feet. Findley scores and Real Salt Lake has taken the lead! The crowd has gone wild. Alvarez goes inside, but there's no space. Cooper almost gets there. Rasha is active tonight. Feeds to Jory. What do you know, Jeff Cunningham is now at the top of the box. There's a scramble and the shot and goal for Jeff Cunningham! That's two goals for him! Rimando didn't see it coming. Dallas ties it up 2–2."

Lacey listened to the announcer, but the play went back and forth so fast, she couldn't keep up. Chaz had brought his binoculars. They would have helped a lot if Abby hadn't wanted to look through them every few minutes. She also moved to the seat below them periodically to sit next to her new friend Cindy.

The noisy crowd was too excited to mind the heat. Between snacks and drinks, and the hugs Abby gave Chaz on impulse, it was clear her daughter was having the time of her life. So was Lacey. She enjoyed his friends, who were fun and friendly.

He leaned close enough to Lacey's ear that she could feel the side of his jaw. The contact sent trickles of delight through her body. "Look at those two little heads of blond and red curls gleaming in the sun like that. What a sight!"

She'd just been thinking the same thing. "Aren't they cute together? But I'm afraid Abby is already turning out to be a social butterfly and she's driving everyone crazy, especially you."

"This is what family life is all about. As you said on your show last night, there's no place I'd rather be than right here, right now."

Maybe she was mistaken, but she thought she heard a throb in his deep voice. It found an echoing chord inside her. While she was immersed in thoughts of him, enjoying the feel of their bodies touching, a huge roar went up from the crowd signaling the end of the soccer match. Some fans started leaving the stands.

"Don't look now, but Real Salt Lake just defeated Dallas. A lot you guys care."

At the sound of Travis's dejected voice directly behind them, Chaz stood up with Lacey and they both turned around. Though Travis's attractive features looked pained by the loss, his eyes were lit up in a smile. "Do you two even know the score?"

"Three to two?" Lacey ventured a lame guess. That was the last she'd heard, but with Chaz sitting next to her, she'd been too distracted to pay much attention.

"Wrong," Travis responded with a devilish grin. "For a brilliant astronomer studying one of Jupiter's moons at my old stomping grounds, I have to admit I'm shocked over your answer, Lacey Pomeroy."

Laughter bubbled out of her. "Blame it on the summer solstice. It's still having its effect on us earthlings."

"I can see that it is," he murmured, eyeing Chaz pointedly. "Maybe that's the reason this old SEAL decided to get himself engaged."

Mitch had been sitting next to Travis, but was now on his feet. "You know what that means? More women for us, even if they are disappointed."

Lacey could well imagine how many women had hoped Chaz would be interested in them. A picture of Ruth's deflated expression over Chaz's disinterest flashed into her mind. As for his friends, he'd warned her about their teasing. "What *are* you guys? The Three Musketeers?"

All three men burst into laughter.

"Sorry I missed out on your show last night," Mitch said after it subsided. "I'd planned to listen, but business interfered. Tonight I'm going to be all ears."

"Tonight would be a good night to tune in. I'll tell Stewart to get you in the lineup if you call in. We're going to have a NASA expert on during the first segment to tell us about UFO reports the government has covered up forever. It ought to be interesting."

"You're right." He was trying hard not to smile, but she could tell he was having a difficult time holding it back.

"It's okay to laugh, Mitch. Chaz doesn't believe in any of it, either, but my feelings aren't hurt. I've studied galaxies trillions and trillions of light-years away.

Earth isn't the only inhabited speck of dust. It couldn't be..." she mused aloud, warming to her favorite topic.

Mitch's appealing face sobered. "I got gooseflesh just then."

"She'll make a believer out of you," Chaz warned as he reached down for Abby and pulled her into his arms. She immediately began patting his cheeks and tried to open the binoculars case.

Lacey took one look and said, "I think it's time my little girl was home in bed." She turned back to Chaz's friends. "This has been loads of fun. I'm so glad I could meet you."

"It's been our pleasure."

The others clustered round. She said goodbye to everyone before they started to make their way to the exit. Over Chaz's shoulder Abby called out, "Bye, Cindy."

"Bye, Abby."

They'd chosen to bring Lacey's car because it had the car seat for Abby. Once she was strapped in, Chaz offered to drive them back to the condo. Lacey liked not having to do the driving all the time. She turned to look at him. "Thank you for a wonderful outing. Abby and I had a marvelous time."

He shot her a glance. "I did, too. That's why it makes what I have to tell you so much harder, but the time has come for you to know the facts on your case. You need to hear them before we get back to your condo." Chaz looked back at Abby. "Don't worry about your daughter hearing us. She's fallen sound asleep."

Lacey's happy smile abruptly vanished.

"I wouldn't be a good P.I. if I didn't do a thorough investigation of every suspect, and that includes your sister."

She clutched her purse. "What about Ruth?"

This was it. "She's been lying to you and your mother."

"How do you know that?"

Naturally her defenses had gone up. "I flew to Idaho Falls and learned she never had a pilot's job with any air cargo company in that region of the state."

"What?"

"She's been living with a pilot by the name of Bruce Larson who works for Landis Air Cargo. They cover routes in all of the western states where your death threats and phone calls could have come from. He lives in an eightplex in Idaho Falls.

"It's the same address she wrote down on the registration form at last year's UFO seminar in Albuquerque. When she left your condo two mornings ago, one of my crew followed her to Salt Lake International airport and she flew in a small plane with him to St. George and back. It's possible she flew there job hunting."

"Oh, Ruth—" Her moan squeezed his heart. By now, Lacey had buried her face in her hands. Though it was killing him, she needed to hear it all.

"She said Shelley Marlow introduced herself at Ted's funeral. But I spoke with your husband's best man, Rob Sharp, and he told me Shelley died from a probable drug overdose two years ago, so she couldn't have been at the funeral."

Lacey was quiet for a long time, then finally lifted her tear-drenched face. "How much more is there?" she asked in a wooden voice.

"I need you to tell me." He pulled a small photograph from his shirt pocket and handed it to her. "That's a picture I took when I was helping Abby try to find her teeny baby in her big-girl bag. Do you recognize the GoPhone among her small toys?"

The silence was palpable while she studied it. "No."

"Abby told me she found it in Auntie Ruth's closet. I'd give you the phone, but it's still with Roman. He had it traced to the person who bought it. The name that came up was Bruce Larson."

A terrible tension held them both in a vise before she said, "You think *Ruth* is my stalker? *My own sister?*" she cried out.

"Yes."

"I don't believe it. You *can't* think it!"

"Believe me, I don't want to, Lacey. You have no idea how much I don't. Remember there are other suspects who have motive and opportunity. I'm waiting on positive proof."

"What proof?" The question came out more like a hiss.

"I took the note and envelope you were sent from the Albuquerque UFO Seminar Committee to the police forensics lab. They couldn't find a fingerprint, but they found two blond-hair samples. I had an expert come to your condo while you weren't home and he went over Ruth's room to get some hair."

Her gasp resounded in the car. "The police came to my home and you didn't tell me?"

"Would you have allowed it?"

Lacey's face closed up, shutting him out.

"By Monday I'll know if your sister's DNA is a match."

Tears gushed down her face as she broke down sobbing. He felt her pain in his gut.

"If it isn't a match, then she's off the suspect list.

Nevertheless she does have serious issues you and your mother should know about for your own peace of mind."

She shook her head. "This just can't be happening. It's going to kill my mother."

"Keep in mind I haven't ruled out Jenny and the other blonds from your group. I still need to keep going with the investigation. That means we'll fly to Albuquerque the way we've planned."

"You expect me to go after what you've just told me?" She looked like a victim of shell shock.

"Yes, because no matter what, you want Abby to be safe. The stalker has to be caught so you don't ever have to be afraid again. You're the strongest woman I've ever met, Lacey Pomeroy. For a little while longer I know you can pretend in front of Ruth and your colleagues that nothing's wrong. I'll be there to protect you and Abby every step of the way."

Lacey remained mute for the rest of the drive to the condo. He parked in her space and shut off the engine. When he looked at her, an expressionless mask had replaced her tears. "I'm sorrier than you will ever know to have been forced to tell you all this, Lacey."

"That's your job," she said in a voice he didn't recognize. "It's why you were hired." He knew she was living a new nightmare. But he was glad that before another minute had gone by, he'd told her what he knew, even if she hated him for it. Oh, yes, she hated him.

"One thing is certain." She climbed out of the car, refusing his help. "Guilty or innocent, I don't want Ruth tending Abby."

Thank heaven Chaz had followed his instincts. "Since she's not here yet, let's hurry inside while you get ready for work. When she arrives, tell her that since we're leaving so early in the morning, we're taking Abby to your mom's on the way to the radio station tonight. That leaves her free to do what she wants. She won't suspect anything's wrong."

Her features hardened. "I hate doing this to Mom, but I have no other choice."

Chaz climbed out and pulled his little butterfly princess from her car seat. She slumped over his shoulder as he carried her up the steps. By the time he unlocked the door, she awakened, wanting some juice.

After a snack it came time for her bath. It turned out to be a quick affair. Jammies followed. Lacey packed a small suitcase for her along with her big-girl bag. Chaz offered to play with her while her mommy got ready for work.

LACEY STEPPED INTO THE shower suffering a pain like she'd never known in her life. Chaz hadn't said Ruth was her stalker, but he'd said he *thought* she was. Much as Lacey didn't want to believe it, her instincts told her he was the best at his job and didn't make mistakes.

Last week he'd suggested that a stalker often had a personality disorder. Was that the reason why Ruth had always been different? In order for her to have written those gruesome thoughts or said them through some voice-distortion device, they had to have sprung from a swirling cauldron in her brain Lacey couldn't comprehend. It saddened and sickened her to think that if it were true, her sister's dark side had manifested itself in a manner that was beyond horrific.

Assuming Ruth was the culprit, how many more threats would her sister make before she took action?

Chaz had said that most female stalkers didn't make physical attacks on their victims. But what if Ruth didn't fit the norm? To think that all this month Lacey had left Abby in her sister's care...

Forewarned was forearmed. She'd heard that saying all her life.

You want Abby to be safe. The stalker has to be caught so you don't ever have to be afraid again. You're the strongest woman I've ever met, Lacey Pomeroy. For a little while longer I know you can pretend in front of Ruth and your colleagues that nothing's wrong.

To keep Abby safe, Lacey *would* do anything.

She slipped into a fresh pair of jeans and a short-sleeved knit top in a light blue. While she was brushing her hair, she glanced in the mirror and realized she'd picked up a lot of color sitting in the sun. Her lips felt dry. She applied two coats of peach-bronze lipstick.

Before leaving her room, she phoned her mother and asked her if she would be willing to tend Abby tonight to save them time in the morning. Her mom was wonderful, as always, and told her to bring Abby right over. Lacey kept the call short. The conversation she needed to have with her mother would have to wait a little longer.

She walked through to the family room with Abby's suitcase and big-girl bag. "How come you didn't wear a hat?" That was the first thing to come out of Ruth's mouth. Her sister had arrived while she'd been in the shower. Abby was over on the couch with Chaz, playing with her nesting dolls. "You look like a lobster."

Lacey had put up with her sister's taunts for years. This was nothing new. "I forgot to take one to the game."

Chaz shot her a level glance. "It wouldn't have stayed on your head anyway," he commented. "Abby would have stolen it for herself, wouldn't you, sweetheart?" Chaz had been learning fast about being around a three-year-old.

"How come Abby's still up?"

"Since we're leaving early for Albuquerque in the morning, I'm dropping her off at Mom's tonight. I'm sorry I couldn't have told you any sooner, but it was a last-minute decision. Feel free to do what you want."

Ruth flashed her a strange look. "This works out perfect for me. I was going to tell you my news after you got home from the radio station, but now I won't have to wait. I'm not going to be able to tend Abby for you any longer."

That *was* news. In light of Chaz's revelations, Lacey froze in place. "What do you mean? Did you get a job?"

"No. I'm going to look for one in Denver."

"Denver?"

"Why not? I haven't had any luck here. Don't worry. As long as you don't need me, I'll clean my room and bathroom and leave tonight."

"You mean you're going to drive all night?"

"Sure. I prefer it in order to avoid the summer traffic during the day. Mom will tend Abby until you find another sitter." She disappeared down the hall to her bedroom and shut the door.

Lacey didn't dare comment or look at Chaz, but she knew what he was thinking because the same thoughts flooded her mind. Ruth had no qualms about walking out on Lacey and dumping Abby on their mother without warning. The idea that Lacey's family needed her during this time of crisis didn't even register with

Ruth. Lacey's sister had always been impulsive, but not flighty.

Ruth was on the run. There was something fundamentally off in her brain. It added credibility to Chaz's theory. The fragile thread of hope Lacey had been clinging to, not wanting to believe the truth about her sister, was stretched so thin it was close to nonexistent. Ice filled her veins.

Chaz held the front door for her and they walked out to her car in silence. Once they were on their way to her mom's, he glanced at her. "Whether she's been the one terrifying you or not, it's beginning to make sense why Ruth has held so many jobs in her life. But I know this is tearing you apart."

"For a lot of reasons," she whispered in pain. "There's something wrong with her. She hasn't been the same since Daddy died."

"In what way?"

"She was the baby. I think after he was gone, she lost her security and is still trying to find it, but this behavior isn't normal, even for her."

"I'm sorry, Lacey. Do you think you'll be able to get the same girl to tend who helped you before?"

"No. She's not available, but she has friends. One of them might be willing to fill in short-term."

"What do you mean, short-term?"

"Because I've made the decision to get out of broadcasting. I'm going to call Barry when we get back from Albuquerque and give him my notice."

Lacey heard his sharp intake of breath. "Then you'd be letting the stalker win."

"No, Chaz. That's not my reason. When I first moved back to Salt Lake, Barry talked me into doing the show here. He was very convincing at the time and told me it could be lucrative. I *was* worried about money, but I'm doing fine now."

"There'll never be another Lacey Pomeroy." His voice sounded husky.

"Someone else always comes along. Alicia, the journalist you're going to meet at the seminar, could do a good job. Or Stewart, who wants to be a paranormal radio host badly and would be great at it. In fact, he's going to fill in for me as host tomorrow night. But of course the final decision is up to Barry."

The producer had been incredibly good to her and had gone out on a limb for her by hiring the P.I. agency. Because the stalker hadn't been caught yet, she hoped he'd understand the horrible strain she'd been under and would find a replacement as soon as he could so she could be let out of her contract.

"I'm afraid Mr. Winslow will be beside himself."

"I hope not, but I can't worry about that. Abby's getting older and to be honest, I don't like being so regimented. She'll be grown up before I know it. Already she's asking questions about why I have to leave every night. You don't see her cry while I'm getting ready to go to work, but she does. That's a worry for a little girl. If she had any idea there was a stalker after me, possibly her *aunt*...

"Today at the game I was watching Cindy, and thinking that when she went home tonight, her mother wouldn't be leaving her. She would go to sleep without a care. I wish I could say the same thing for my Abby. I suspect her terror of bees is all part of *her* insecurity.

"Ruth and I lost our father and there was nothing we could do about that. Abby's already lost one parent, but she doesn't have to lose me every weeknight. All I have to do is quit my job. What you've told me about Ruth has clarified my priorities."

They'd arrived at her mother's house. He shut off the engine. "Let me help you."

"Thank you, but no. I'll take her in and be right back."

IT HAD BEGUN. CHAZ FELT HER putting distance between them. By telling her the facts as they had lined up, he'd made his fear of losing her a lot less far-fetched. After she got back into the car, they drove to the radio station in silence.

While she began her broadcast, he planted himself in her office and listened to his phone messages. Chaz figured Ruth would be gone by the time he and Lacey got back to the condo. Anticipating as much, he phoned Lon and Jim on a conference call because he needed Ruth followed wherever she went.

"The situation has changed, guys. Lacey's sister won't be staying nights at the condo any longer. Don't let her out of your sight." He left it to the two of them to coordinate with each other. "If you need more help, call Lyle."

Ruth's sudden decision to look for work in Denver didn't ring true with Chaz any more than it had with Lacey. She was in too big a hurry to leave Salt Lake. He didn't trust her. That Bruce Larson had bought the phone Ruth had used underscored the fact that she and the pilot had some kind of secret relationship going on.

Any way you looked at it, the situation was ugly and getting uglier by the second. Somewhere in all this lay the truth, with Ruth and her boyfriend in the mix. Chaz was so close he could taste it.

Having done all the business he could for the moment, he joined Stewart to listen to and watch Lacey through the glass. Her ability to carry on in such a courageous manner impressed him beyond words. Chaz could only do so much to make her feel safe. He couldn't get inside her mind and ease her pain over her sister.

When she introduced her NASA guest Richard Fulquist on the last segment of the show, she said, "Richard, there are always those in the audience who take a cynical view of what you'll be talking about tonight. One of them could be listening, so I'll say hello to Mitch, who missed out on last night's program, but said he'd arrange to be 'all ears' tonight."

Chaz hoped Mitch had tuned in to her program. He'd noticed her visual impact on his friends, but he knew hearing her in action on a subject she loved made the fascination with her grow to a whole new dimension.

To his amusement, her last caller before she went off the air was Mitch. "Tell your producer thanks for letting me get in a final word. The conversation with your NASA guest has caused me to rethink certain opinions, and that doesn't happen very often.

"If I may quote what was said at the beginning of your show, you managed to open my mind to all the possibilities in an unending number of universes. For those who would love to see me eat crow, and you know who you are, you've gotten your wish."

Mitch couldn't have made it any plainer he was talking to Chaz, who smiled to himself before Lacey came out of the booth. But she wasn't the same woman who'd kissed him with passion the other night. This woman was the professional who said good-night to everyone and walked out to the car without waiting for him to help her.

After they got into the car he started the engine, then turned to her. "Thanks for making Mitch's night."

"I'm glad he called in." With that comment, she remained quiet for the drive home. When they reached the complex, there was no sign of Ruth's car. They went inside, and without looking at him Lacey said, "Let's grab what sleep we can."

He nodded. "Five-thirty is going to come fast. Good night, Lacey."

"Good night."

Everything about the situation was tearing him up. Much as he wanted to comfort her, he couldn't do that. Not until he could prove the stalker's identity, so the harassment would stop.

He turned on his heel and headed for the deck. A man could take only so much. He got ready for bed and lay down. As his mind went over everything he knew about Ruth, he found himself breaking out in a cold sweat. There'd be no sleep for him tonight.

When he brought his bag and mattress into the kitchen the next morning, he discovered Lacey at the sink. She'd dressed in a soft yellow two-piece suit with a silky white blouse. On her feet she wore white heels that added two inches to her height.

He locked the sliding door. She heard the noise and turned to him, causing her red hair to settle like a cloud at her shoulders. Her beauty disarmed him, but she was in tears and looked as if she hadn't slept, either.

"What is it?"

"I called my mom and told her we would drop by before we left for the airport. I need to see Abby."

"Of course."

He carried their bags out to her car and made their way to her mother's house. En route his phone rang. It was Lon reporting in.

"What's happening, Lon?"

"Ms. Garvey didn't head for Denver. She's about a half hour away from Idaho Falls. I'm a few car lengths behind her."

That didn't surprise Chaz. She was getting back to her boyfriend as fast as possible. "Stay on it and keep me posted."

He pulled into the driveway and helped Lacey from the car. The minute they went inside the house, Lacey's mother noticed the difference in her. "What's wrong, honey?"

"Everything." She hugged her mother for a long time. Chaz felt a swelling in his throat.

"Let's talk in the living room while Abby's still asleep."

Chaz sat in an easy chair while Lacey sat on the couch with Virginia. "Mom? Have you heard from Ruth or seen her since yesterday?"

"No. Why?"

Lacey's face blanched. "Because last night she quit her job with me and said she was driving to Denver to look for work."

The older woman looked shocked. "Denver?"

"Oh, Mom…there's something terribly, terribly wrong with her. Chaz has found things out about her while he's been doing his investigation. She's been living with that guy Bruce she sometimes talks to on the phone. Chaz found out she never did get a pilot's job while she was in Idaho Falls. Whatever has been going on, it's not good. I'm sick to my stomach over her."

"So am I, darling." Her mother jumped up from the couch. "She's been distant and secretive since your father passed away. Since Ted died, she's been even worse. I haven't known what to do, but I can't let this go on any longer. No matter how much she doesn't want me interfering, if I knew where to find her in Denver, I'd go after her."

"I know where to find her, Virginia." Chaz couldn't keep quiet any longer. "She's in Idaho."

Both women stared at him in surprise. The hurt look in Lacey's eyes gutted him all over again.

"As you know, I've been keeping all of you under surveillance for your protection and one of my men tracked her there. You're welcome to talk to Lon. He'll help you in any way you want." Chaz wrote down Lon's cell phone number and gave it to her.

"If you decide you'd like to drive or fly to Idaho, he'll be happy to meet you and drive you to her. He'll stay with you the entire time. Lacey and I would go with you, but I'm still working Lacey's case and it's critical we show up to that seminar. We'll take Abby with us."

The silence was palpable. "Why don't you two talk for a minute," he suggested. "Lacey? I'm going out to the car and making another seat reservation for Abby. We only need to stay at the seminar long enough for me to conduct my investigation, then we'll fly back tonight instead of Sunday."

Her lovely features had hardened. She nodded before turning to her mother. "I think you ought to go to Idaho,

Mom. I've never been able to get through to Ruth, but I know *you* can. Chaz has promised you full protection. I'll get Abby ready."

Chapter Eleven

During the hour-and-a-half flight to Albuquerque, Lacey's whole attention was focused on Abby. Chaz had to sit farther down the aisle. Brenda sat in the opposite direction from Chaz. Lacey was thankful she didn't have to talk to either of them. She couldn't.

"Oh, Abby," she whispered in torment, rocking her daughter back and forth. Her mother shouldn't have to face Ruth alone, but Lacey knew there was a side of her sister that hated Lacey in a way that knew no boundaries. Her mother would have better luck confronting her on her own.

What if Ruth really was the stalker?

Lacey must have asked herself that question a dozen times in the limo on the way to the hotel. Brenda kept up a running commentary with Chaz, unaware she was doing Lacey a favor. If she talked to him right now, she might have hysterics.

Thankfully she and Abby were swarmed by convention-goers the moment she approached the hall table to get her name tag. Jenny hadn't arrived yet. Brenda created an explosion of excitement when she announced to the UFO committee that Lacey was engaged, and the gorgeous guy with the black hair she had in tow was none other than her fiancé, Chaz Roylance.

Every female attendee within viewing distance zeroed in on him. Why not. Having been blessed with a tall, rip cord–strong physique and rugged features arranged to stop a woman in her tracks, he looked exceptionally fantastic in a tan suit and white open-necked sport shirt.

She watched him charm her core group of friends, who'd assembled around her. He'd studied the background on each one and knew what to say to draw them out. Ken was conspicuously absent, something Chaz would have noticed immediately. When the announcement came over the loudspeaker that the seminar was about to begin, he moved closer.

His eyes played over her in a way that said he liked what he was seeing. But maybe all this was for show. She didn't know what was real anymore. "If you'll let me take Abby, I'm going to walk her around and get her something to eat in the restaurant. We'll come in and out to see you, but this is your day to enjoy yourself, so take advantage of me."

After having gone to the extent of pretending to be engaged, Lacey couldn't very well say no to him in front of her friends who were listening. With Abby in his arms, he had the legitimate right to circulate and study the crowd. Her stomach clenched to realize he was here to meet Jenny, the second suspect on his list.

"That would be wonderful. I'll just take her to the little girls' room, then we'll be right back."

When she returned, Chaz plucked Abby from her arms. "Come on, sweetheart. Let's go look around."

Her cute little red head peered over his broad shoulder. "Okay. Bye, Mommy. Don't go away."

"I'll be right here."

Lacey purposely chose an aisle seat near the back of the conference room. She saved the two seats next to her for Chaz to have easy access. But from the moment the key speaker started the program, her brain was trying to fathom Ruth's troubled mind instead of concentrating on the latest UFO sightings throughout the world in the past month.

With her body in a fight-or-flight mode, she sat rigidly in her seat studying the faces of her friends. By the time lunch was announced and the divider removed for them to take their places at the tables, her nerves were shot. She was grateful for a glass of water to take a painkiller for her full-on headache.

"Lacey!" Jenny cried and rushed around the table to hug her. "My flight got in late. Where's your fiancé? I'm dying to meet him."

Her blonde friend wouldn't be so eager if she knew Chaz had suspected her from the very first. "He's taken Abby for a walk."

"You brought Abby?"

"Yes. I didn't want to leave her."

By now the chicken-and-rice entrée was being brought to the tables. "I don't blame you. Oh, I can't wait to see her." She sat down next to her. "When are you getting married?"

"That's what *I* want to know." Brenda had just joined them.

"I-it's too soon to make plans," Lacey stammered. "Abby needs time to get used to him being around for a while. I have to be sure." Though the lie was still necessary, Lacey hated this subterfuge with every fiber of her being.

"That's what engagements are for," Jenny whispered. "You can always break them and there'll be no harm done. My husband didn't want us to get engaged. Like a fool, I thought *how romantic* and dived into the deep end of marriage headfirst." Her eyes watered. "If I'd had your smarts, I would have insisted on an engagement. It would have saved me a lot of grief."

"Mommy."

Lacey swung her head around. In that brief instant she glanced up at Chaz, who held Abby in his arms. But his attention was focused on Jenny. The sheer intensity of his stare sent a chill down Lacey's spine.

"Come here, honey." She reached for her daughter, needing the comfort of her little body close to stop the tremors. "Chaz? I'd like you to meet Jennifer West, my other closest friend in the world. Jenny? This is Chaz Roylance."

He flashed that bone-melting smile he wasn't aware of. "At last we meet."

Jenny's gaze had leveled on Chaz. Like every woman, she was struck by his dark good looks. It was there in her eyes, still guarded by a layer of distrust of men in general. "I understand congratulations are in order. Lacey's one in a million."

"You don't have to tell me that. I knew the moment I started reading her Stargrazer novel." Chaz sat down on the other side of Jenny—it was the only empty chair.

Lacey hadn't meant for them to get separated. Jenny hugged Abby and didn't seem to notice or jump up to change places. Lacey was glad. Sitting next to him wouldn't be a good idea. Her pain and fear over what was happening in Idaho made it impossible to talk to him, so it was better they couldn't.

"I've been curious about something. When did you girls first learn she'd had a book published?" Chaz had thrown the question out there. He could have asked them anything. Why he'd brought up that subject baffled her.

"Mrs. Garvey told us. But we knew about everything from Rita."

"Rita?" Chaz questioned.

"The school librarian. We were all friends with her and she told us Lacey was looking for a publisher."

Brenda nodded. "We knew she'd been writing a novel about Percy."

"*How* did you know that?" Lacey couldn't believe it and stared at them in total astonishment.

They both burst into laughter before Jenny said, "We always saw you working on it in class while you were supposed to be studying. At the slumber party for your birthday, you fell asleep. We found your looseleaf and took turns reading it. If you hadn't sent it in to get published, we would have done it for you. It was that good!"

"The only thing I didn't like was the ending," Brenda blurted.

"Neither did I," Chaz interjected. "Why didn't *you* like it?"

Brenda winked at him. "Why do you think? She'd written it for young adults, so the part we adult girls were all waiting for never came."

That got to Chaz. He let go with his rich laughter, and a laughing Chaz rocked Lacey to her foundation. It caught Abby's attention. She wiggled away and ran to him. He pulled her onto his lap. "Help me finish my lunch. What does my butterfly princess want?"

"Cake!"

While everyone at the table laughed, Brenda eyed Lacey. "Butterfly princess?" she mouthed the words.

Lacey smiled. She had to admit it was pretty cute. More than cute. He was so wonderful with Abby, she had to look away while she choked down the little sob that rose in her throat. She'd been so blindsided by Chaz that first night, she hadn't seen he was first and foremost a professional P.I. just doing his job.

Her little offshoot, Abby, was no different. Chaz had gotten to her, too. But Lacey could feel things were coming to an end. In a few hours they'd be flying back to Salt Lake. She hadn't heard from her mother yet, but feared the news about Ruth couldn't be good.

Chaz had been the one who'd uncovered everything and was waiting for the results of the DNA match.

Her breath was trapped painfully in her chest. Her mother shouldn't have had to go to Idaho alone, she thought again. If there were no stalker... But there was, and Chaz had been working her case nonstop. She should be feeling nothing but gratitude, but human nature was more complicated than that. Her deepest emotions were confused and complicated.

More anxious by the moment, she excused herself from the table and took Abby to the ladies' room. From there she walked her outside for a minute and phoned her mom. When there was no response, she left a message for her to call.

As she turned to go back inside, she almost ran into Chaz, who'd come out the doors. He took one look at her and demanded to know what was wrong.

"I haven't been able to reach my mother yet."

He grimaced before examining her upturned features. "Are you getting anything out of this conference?"

"No," she answered woodenly. "I came because you said we should come."

His mouth tautened. "I've seen what I needed to see. Let's head to the airport. We might be able to get on an earlier flight back to Salt Lake. I'll arrange it."

"I—I need to say goodbye to my friends," her voice faltered.

"I'll run inside and tell them Abby's too restless and we need to go. They'll all understand. You find us a cab."

She nodded.

"Chaz!" Abby called to him. "Stay here."

"I'll be right back, sweetheart."

Stay here.

Lacey wondered how long her daughter would ask for Chaz after he'd gone out of their lives. In her heart she knew he'd be going soon.

Just now he'd told her he'd seen what he needed to see. At his office last week he'd said the next step would be to bring in the police so an arrest could be made.

Chaz had promised to keep her and Abby safe. So far he'd kept his word. He'd asked her to trust him. He'd said the pseudo engagement would produce results sooner.

When she thought back to the day Barry had first hired a P.I. from the Lufka firm, she couldn't imagine anything coming of it. Yet nine days later, it appeared Chaz had accomplished the impossible.

But not without collateral damage.

Her heart thudded painfully. Her mom hadn't called yet. Lacey was growing more and more anxious over Ruth's lies. So many of them. Such serious ones. Had she really sent that fax and left those evil phone messages?

AFTER TOUCHING DOWN AT Salt Lake International at six-thirty, they drove to Mrs. Garvey's house. Chaz had called Lon to find out about Mrs. Garvey, but their call had been dropped driving through a non-service area. As they pulled up in the driveway, he saw Lacey's mother appear on the front porch.

"Oh, I'm so glad you're back." She came hurrying to Lacey's side of the car.

"Did you talk to her, Mom?"

"No. After discussing everything with Lon, I decided to wait. They're keeping a close eye on Ruth." She looked inside the car at Chaz. "He felt you should be the one to discuss everything with me and Lacey after you got back."

He nodded. "We'll do it as soon as I check in at my office. It won't take long. Is that all right with you, Lacey?"

"Yes," she said without looking at him. "Take my car. Mom can drive me home in hers. She has a car seat for Abby. I have to get her ready for bed."

"I'll hurry," he murmured.

Abby started crying. "Stay here, Chaz."

"I'll be back, sweetheart."

He had to harden himself against her tears. After backing Lacey's car down the driveway to the street, he headed for work. It wasn't far away.

The place was as quiet as a tomb. He guessed everyone was either out working on their cases, or done for the evening. Someone had put a fax from the crime lab on his desk. He picked it up.

> Mr. Roylance. Because this is a stalking case, I knew you wanted this info ASAP. Won't send complete printout now, but there was a match on the hair samples from the envelope and the DNA found in the bedroom. Hope this helps your case. S. Evans

For a brief moment Chaz felt exultation that Ruth had been conclusively identified. Lacey and Abby were no longer in danger. But his emotion was short-lived because of what he had to do now.

Do you like your job?

Ruth had asked him that question several days ago. He squeezed his eyes tightly for a minute. After pulling himself together, he checked in with Lon. "What's the status on Ruth?"

"Except to go out for a hamburger, she's been in Larson's apartment since she got here. He hasn't shown up yet. Jim drove up and we're spelling each other off. Where are you?"

"Back in Salt Lake. I just got the proof I've been waiting for. Ruth Garvey is Lacey's stalker."

"Oh, boy," Lon muttered.

"If her boyfriend has been in on it, the police will learn soon enough. I'm phoning Roman now to get hold of the authorities in Idaho Falls to make the arrest. Then I'll be on my way over to Lacey's condo to give her and her mother the bad news. Once I know how they want to proceed, you'll hear from me. Thanks for the great work, Lon. I'll let the guys on surveillance know it's over."

"I don't envy you for what you have to do."

Chaz didn't even want to think about it.

THE NEXT AFTERNOON CHAZ met Lacey and her mother at police headquarters in Salt Lake. Virginia did all the talking as he ushered them into the detective's office. He learned that Julie Howard, the girl across the street from the Garveys, had agreed to tend Abby for the day. Lacey said nothing to him. She wouldn't even look at him.

Ruth and Bruce had both been arrested. He was being held in Idaho Falls while a full investigation was carried out. Ruth had been transferred to Salt Lake. At the moment, she was being held in jail prior to arraignment before a judge.

Roman had given Chaz the name of an excellent defense attorney, Art Walker. Virginia had already talked to Mr. Walker and he'd been willing to take Ruth's case. This would be Lacey and her mother's first chance to talk to Ruth. Their haunted expressions as they left the room with the detective devastated Chaz.

After they'd gone, he pulled out his cell and phoned the office. Lisa answered. "Roman told me you did an amazing job of investigative work," she said.

"So amazing Lacey can't even look at me right now."

"She's working through a living death, but it will pass."

"I need to do the same thing. Will you put Roman on? I'd like to get out of town for a while to clear my head."

"I'll let him know you're on the phone. Hold on."

Ruth sat in a chair behind a desk wearing jail garb. When she saw Lacey and their mother, she smiled. The two of them sat down. Once the guard closed the door she said, "I'll admit Chaz knows his stuff, Lacey. You do manage to pick the studs."

Her mother leaned forward. "We've hired an attorney for you, honey. His name is Art Walker. He's going to help you."

"Nobody can help me. If Dad were here…but he isn't. No one else ever loved me."

"From what I've learned, Bruce Larson loves you and has been taking care of you for a long time."

"Until he found out I was using him. Then he broke up with me. I drove back to Idaho to tell him I wouldn't play those tricks on Lacey anymore, but he doesn't believe me. He's not Dad. No one is. You lucked out, too, Mom. You and Lacey…you always land on your feet."

Lacey's pain for her sister cut deep.

"I never would have hurt you or Abby, Lacey. I was only playing a joke because your world has always been so perfect. Then your navy SEAL moved in and ruined everything. I tried to put the moves on him like I did with Ted, but neither of them took the bait."

She'd been attracted to Ted, too? Lacey tried to absorb it all, but it was too heartbreaking.

"I'm not like either one of you, but Dad thought I was beautiful and wonderful. I wish he hadn't died." After saying that, she just sat there staring at the table, as if she were in another world.

"Do you want us to stay with you?" their mother asked, but Ruth didn't answer. The minutes ticked by before Virginia patted Lacey's arm. "Let's go," she whispered.

They got up. Her mother knocked on the door and the guard let them out. When they were alone in the hall she looked at Lacey through pain-filled eyes. "She needs psychiatric care."

Lacey nodded. "I had no idea the damage Dad's death did to her."

"Neither of us realized. Maybe a good doctor can tell us why. Let's go to Mr. Walker's office and find out what happens next."

They left the police station. Lacey looked everywhere, but Chaz had disappeared. She shouldn't have been surprised. His job was done and he'd probably gone back to the office to get started on his next case. Lacey felt as if she'd just fallen into a black void.

Chapter Twelve

By the time Lacey pulled up in front of the Lufka P.I. firm a week later, her whole body was trembling. She walked inside on unsteady legs. Lisa, the woman she'd met at the soccer game, was sitting at the front desk. When she looked up and saw who it was, she got to her feet and came around to give Lacey a hug. "I'm so sorry about your sister."

"So am I. She's finally getting the therapy she needs, so that's something anyway."

"Of course it is. What can I do for you?"

"Is Chaz going to be coming in? I didn't see his car out in back."

"I'm sorry, but he's on vacation."

The news sent her heart plummeting. "Do you know how much longer he'll be gone?"

"I don't, but when he calls in, I'll let him know you were asking for him."

"No…that's okay. Thanks, Lisa." As she started to leave, she heard her name called and turned around. "Mitch…"

He hurried toward her. "The second I saw a flash of red hair, I knew it couldn't belong to anyone else." His eyes looked at her with compassion. "I'm sorry to hear about your sister."

"Me, too, but she's in custody under psychiatric care now and with time I know she's going to get a lot better. I was hoping to talk to Chaz. It's been a week since I last saw him at police headquarters. I need to thank him."

"I'm sure he'll appreciate that."

It was impossible to swallow when her mouth had gone dry. "Do you know when he'll be back?"

"No, but if it's any help, he told us where he could be reached if an emergency came up." He stared hard at her. "Is this an emergency?"

She knew what he was asking. It was a time for honesty. "Yes. My daughter asks for him constantly."

Mitch's eyes softened. "He's staying at the Old Miner bed-and-breakfast in Deer Valley for a little R & R."

Lacey hadn't heard of it, but there were a lot of new places being built up there. She'd find it. "Thank you, Mitch." She gave him a hug before hurrying out to her car.

A half hour's drive in the mountains and she came to the charming Swiss chalet–type retreat. The man at the front desk nodded to her. "I can save you the trouble of asking for a room. We're a small establishment and are filled up until the middle of August. I'm sorry."

"Actually, I'm here to see a guest. His name is Chaz Roylance."

"He went out after breakfast and hasn't returned. If you'd like to leave a message on the phone…"

"I'll write him a note instead." She sat down on one

of the armchairs in the small lounge off the foyer and pulled pen and paper from her purse.

Olivia got separated from Percy after they reached Algol. She's going to die in the rarified atmosphere if he doesn't find her quick and revive her. He has the only antidote.

Lacey got up and handed the paper to the desk manager. "Will you put this in his box?"

He nodded.

"Is it all right if I wait here?"

"Of course. Help yourself to coffee or tea."

"Thank you."

She had no idea how long Chaz would be out, but it didn't matter. Jenny was still in Salt Lake and had begged to tend Abby today. She'd insisted it would help get her mind off her father, who was going through a hard time with his chemo treatment.

Twenty minutes later Lacey sucked in her breath when she saw Chaz's dark head. He strode swiftly through the foyer dressed in jeans and a black polo.

"Mr. Roylance," the concierge called to him. "I have a message for you."

His expression fierce, he backtracked long enough to take the note before disappearing down the hall without a word.

Wondering what he would do after he read it, Lacey's heart pounded so hard she had to get to her feet. Thankfully she didn't have to wait long to find out. He was back at the desk in a flash. "Where's the redheaded woman who delivered this message?"

"I'm right here."

He spun around, out of breath. There were brackets around his mouth. She could tell he'd been suffering, but his fabulous eyes flew over her, taking on that green-and-yellow glow. It was like that night at the radio station when they'd first seen each other. She couldn't breathe then, either.

"Lacey..." He groaned her name.

She shook her head. "I don't know why you've stayed away, but I couldn't take it any longer. Mitch told me where to find you. Do you mind?"

Chaz let out a frustrated laugh. "Mind? Just now I came back here to check out and come find you. We have to talk."

"I agree." She closed the distance between them. "You think Mom and I don't know how hard this was for you? You're my hero, Chaz. We're both so grateful to you, and now it's over. My sister is finally getting the help she's needed for years. Bruce was innocent in all this, and he's standing by her. Now it's time for us. Let's go somewhere private."

He rubbed the back of his neck, as if he needed to do something with his hands. "Where's Abby?"

"With Jenny. Since you've been gone, she's been the unhappiest little butterfly I've ever seen. 'Where's Chaz?' she keeps asking me. I've been asking the same thing. Whatever has put you in this dark place, I'm here for you."

She felt his hand reach for hers and squeeze it so hard, she realized he didn't know his own strength. "My room's at the end of the hall. If you come in, I won't let you out."

"Why do you think Olivia went to Algol with Percy?"

"You'll have to tell me," his voice grated. "You cheated this adult out of the end of the story I was waiting for, remember?"

"Let's get away from prying eyes first," she whispered.

He pulled her along with him. The second they were inside the room, he pressed her against the closed door with his body. Both their hearts were racing. "You're still wearing the ring," he said against her lips.

"Since I got to Algol, it won't come off. It's grown onto my finger."

"That's good because those diamonds are real."

"*That's* why they dazzle my eyes. But real or fake, I'm in love with you, Chaz. Why have you stayed away?"

"Because I should have given your case to one of the other guys the second I suspected your sister. I was afraid I'd ruined my chances with you. To hear about Ruth from me must have been so traumatic, I wouldn't have blamed you if you despised me forever."

"How could I do that? I admit it was horrible to learn the truth, but it wasn't your fault, darling. Why would you think that?"

"In the SEALs we had orders to kill the enemy, but there was a time when I came face-to-face with women brandishing automatic weapons. It made me ill to do my job. So ill I had to get out. I promised I'd never put myself in a position of facing a female enemy again.

"I thought I was safe being a P.I. When I asked to take your case, it was because I thought it was a man stalking you. I wanted to protect you and Abby. It made me feel good for the first time since leaving the service. But the signs kept pointing to a woman. Your sister—

I didn't know if she carried a weapon. I didn't want to find out. I couldn't bear the thought that I might have to shoot her to protect you."

"Oh, darling…" She wrapped her arms around his neck and clung to him. "You *did* protect me. You made me feel safe from the moment we met at the radio station. If it weren't for you, Ruth might have gotten much worse with time. Hearing what you've just told me, I love you more for having taken that risk for me."

She covered his face with kisses. "I love you, Chaz. No other man will ever measure up to you. I need you. Abby needs you."

"Talk about needing…" He devoured her mouth until she was gasping for breath. "How long are you going to keep me waiting to marry you?"

"I don't want to wait. Everyone thinks we've known each other for a year anyway and they won't question it. In case you didn't know, I'm off the radio and a free woman. Barry's giving Stewart a try." She tasted his mouth over and over again.

"I need to do something spectacular for that man. When he went to your firm for help, he had no idea it would produce the real Percy who'd been living in my heart for years."

Chaz crushed her in his arms. "I adore you, Lacey, and couldn't love Abby more if she were my own child."

"I know you mean that, but just wait till you have one of your own, hopefully with black hair. Abby needs a sibling. What do you think?"

He cupped her face in his hands. "I think the gates of paradise just opened."

"Now you know the end of my story. But it's really

only the beginning of a new one, unfolding in a universe expanding with new possibilities. That is, if we ever stop talking."

As he picked her up and swung her around, the last sound she heard was Chaz's laughter, the most beautiful sound in the world.

* * * * *

HEART & HOME

Heartwarming romances where love can
happen right when you least expect it.

Harlequin

American Romance

COMING NEXT MONTH
AVAILABLE FEBRUARY 14, 2012

#1389 ARIZONA COWBOY
Rodeo Rebels
Marin Thomas

#1390 RANCHER DADDY
Saddler's Prairie
Ann Roth

#1391 THE RODEO MAN'S DAUGHTER
Fatherhood
Barbara White Daille

#1392 THE DETECTIVE'S ACCIDENTAL BABY
Safe Harbor Medical
Jacqueline Diamond

REQUEST YOUR FREE BOOKS!
2 FREE NOVELS PLUS 2 FREE GIFTS!

♦Harlequin®

American ★ *Romance*®

LOVE, HOME & HAPPINESS

YES! Please send me 2 FREE Harlequin® American Romance® novels and my 2 FREE gifts (gifts are worth about $10). After receiving them, if I don't wish to receive any more books, I can return the shipping statement marked "cancel." If I don't cancel, I will receive 4 brand-new novels every month and be billed just $4.49 per book in the U.S. or $5.24 per book in Canada. That's a saving of at least 14% off the cover price! It's quite a bargain! Shipping and handling is just 50¢ per book in the U.S. and 75¢ per book in Canada.* I understand that accepting the 2 free books and gifts places me under no obligation to buy anything. I can always return a shipment and cancel at any time. Even if I never buy another book, the two free books and gifts are mine to keep forever.

154/354 HDN FEP2

Name	(PLEASE PRINT)	
Address		Apt. #
City	State/Prov.	Zip/Postal Code

Signature (if under 18, a parent or guardian must sign)

Mail to the **Reader Service:**
IN U.S.A.: P.O. Box 1867, Buffalo, NY 14240-1867
IN CANADA: P.O. Box 609, Fort Erie, Ontario L2A 5X3

Not valid for current subscribers to Harlequin American Romance books.

Want to try two free books from another line?
Call 1-800-873-8635 or visit www.ReaderService.com.

* Terms and prices subject to change without notice. Prices do not include applicable taxes. Sales tax applicable in N.Y. Canadian residents will be charged applicable taxes. Offer not valid in Quebec. This offer is limited to one order per household. All orders subject to credit approval. Credit or debit balances in a customer's account(s) may be offset by any other outstanding balance owed by or to the customer. Please allow 4 to 6 weeks for delivery. Offer available while quantities last.

Your Privacy—The Reader Service is committed to protecting your privacy. Our Privacy Policy is available online at www.ReaderService.com or upon request from the Reader Service.

We make a portion of our mailing list available to reputable third parties that offer products we believe may interest you. If you prefer that we not exchange your name with third parties, or if you wish to clarify or modify your communication preferences, please visit us at www.ReaderService.com/consumerschoice or write to us at Reader Service Preference Service, P.O. Box 9062, Buffalo, NY 14269. Include your complete name and address.

HARI1B

Harlequin

Super Romance

Discover a touching new trilogy from
USA TODAY bestselling author

Janice Kay Johnson

Between Love and Duty

As the eldest brother of three, Duncan MacLachlan
is used to being in control and maintaining an
emotional distance; as a police captain it's his job.
But when he meets Jane Brooks, Duncan soon finds
his control slipping away. Together, they fight for a
young boy's future, and soon Duncan finds himself
hoping to build a future with Jane.

Available February 2012

From Father to Son
(March 2012)

The Call of Bravery
(April 2012)

*Louisa Morgan loves being around children.
So when she has the opportunity to tutor bedridden Ellie,
she's determined to bring joy back into the motherless
girl's world. Can she also help Ellie's father open his
heart again? Read on for a sneak peek of*

THE COWBOY FATHER

*by Linda Ford,
available February 2012 from Love Inspired Historical.*

Why had Louisa thought she could do this job? A bubble of self-pity whispered she was totally useless, but Louisa ignored it. She wasn't useless. She could help Ellie if the child allowed it.

Emmet walked her out, waiting until they were out of earshot to speak. "I sense you and Ellie are not getting along."

"Ellie has lost her freedom. On top of that, everything is new. Familiar things are gone. Her only defense is to exert what little independence she has left. I believe she will soon tire of it and find there are more enjoyable ways to pass the time."

He looked doubtful. Louisa feared he would tell her not to return. But after several seconds' consideration, he sighed heavily. "You're right about one thing. She's lost everything. She can hardly be blamed for feeling out of sorts."

"She hasn't lost everything, though." Her words were quiet, coming from a place full of certainty that Emmet was more than enough for this child. "She has you."

"She'll always have me. As long as I live." He clenched his fists. "And I fully intend to raise her in such a way that even if something happened to me, she would never feel like I was gone. I'd be in her thoughts and in her actions